HER BIG CITY NEIGHBOR

CIDER BAR SISTERS, BOOK 1

JACKIE LAU

First edition: September 2020
ISBN: 978-1-989610-17-6

Editor: Latoya C. Smith, LCS Literary Services

Cover Design: Flirtation Designs

Cover photograph: Adobe Stock

[1]

AMY SHARPE STOOD on the sidewalk and surveyed the narrow, semi-detached Victorian house. It had reddish-brown brick and blue trim, and a tiny garden out front.

And it was, unbelievably, hers. All hers.

She grinned.

Then she felt bad for smiling. The reason she owned this house was that Great Aunt Frances had died six months ago and left it to her.

Amy glanced down at the sidewalk and said a silent prayer of thanks to her great aunt before looking up again.

She'd been shocked that she'd inherited the house. She'd only met Aunt Frances—her paternal grandmother's sister—maybe half a dozen times. Real estate was not cheap in Canada's biggest city, and Amy had nearly fainted when she'd discovered how much this house was worth. She'd known houses were expensive in Toronto, but…wow.

Many times more than what a house would be worth in her small hometown near Sudbury. But there were no Victorian houses back home.

Speaking of back home…her mom was calling.

Amy answered. "Hi, Mom."

"Hi, sweetie. Everything go okay? You're all moved in?"

"Yep, the moving truck just left. It hardly looks like I have any stuff when it's spread out in a three-story house, but it's all here."

"That's good." A pause. "I'll let you go now. I'm sure you have lots of unpacking to do."

That was a remarkably short phone call for her mother, and though Mom had sounded upbeat, Amy knew her mother wasn't thrilled with the move.

Amy had finished her degree eight years ago. She'd planned to work for a few years, then go to grad school. Live somewhere big and exciting.

But then, well, shit happened.

Specifically, her beloved grandmother got sick.

And so Amy had moved back to Silver River and gotten a job as an engineer in Sudbury. She was glad she'd been there for the last two years of her grandmother's life. It was worth delaying her plans.

At twenty-four, she'd started to consider her options, thinking maybe she'd try to get a job in Ottawa or Toronto, and then she'd met a guy, who lived just on the other side of Sudbury.

So, once again, Amy had stayed.

That relationship had lasted longer than it should have, until almost a year ago.

A few months later, she'd inherited this house, and it was like a sign. Amy didn't really believe in signs...

Okay, she totally did.

This inheritance was a sign that it was time for her to leave. She'd never even considered selling it. With this house, she could afford to live in downtown Toronto and go back to school—the university was within walking distance. She'd applied to a master's program in the Department of Civil Engineering, and she may have jumped up and down when she got in.

Thank you, Aunt Frances.

Now it was the end of July, and it was time to start her new life.

She squealed and clapped her hands, trying not to think of her mom's disapproving look when she'd told her of these plans several months ago.

A man walking by with a dog gave her a weird look, but that was okay. She didn't know him. How exciting to be in a new city, where she didn't know anyone! Where her family couldn't pop in uninvited and ask her to run errands or babysit. Where her neighbors hadn't known her all her life.

In fact, she knew no one in Toronto. There were a bunch of classmates from Queen's University, but she hadn't seen them in eight years. They didn't really count.

But she would make friends. She was good at that sort of thing…wasn't she? It had been a while since she'd been anywhere new.

And for the rest of today, she would explore.

She'd done research on nearby shops and restaurants. This area was apparently called the Annex. She wasn't sure why—something to look up when she got the chance.

She went upstairs and had a shower, then put on a sunflower halter dress that she thought was pretty cute. Not that she was meeting anyone, but she felt like looking pretty all the same. She stuffed her wallet, phone, and the latest Sierra Wu book into her purse and walked out the front door.

Which she should lock. Right.

There was a spring in her step as she headed to Harbord Street, just a short walk away. She knew exactly where she was going first: Harbord Coffee Bar.

She'd been intrigued when she'd looked at the website last week. In Silver River, there was only a Tim Hortons, no Starbucks or Second Cup. Certainly nothing that would call itself a "coffee bar."

Her father would think it was dreadfully pretentious. As

would Shane. But Shane thought a man cooking dinner was pretentious, so his opinions didn't matter anymore.

But what intrigued Amy the most was that Harbord Coffee Bar had Japanese-style desserts. What would those be like?

The aroma of coffee hit her as she stepped inside. It was a minimalist design with lots of pale wood. To the right was the counter with a glass display case full of gorgeous pastries. Amy carefully read the description of each one. There were roll cakes, which seemed to be their specialty, plus cheesecake, cream puffs, and things she'd never seen before.

"Can I help you?" asked the lady behind the counter. Her nametag said "Lucy."

Amy shot her a smile. "Just deciding."

She let four people order before her. How was she supposed to decide when everything looked so good? One of the roll cakes had strawberries and whipped cream. It looked delicious, but no, she would try something *different*. Maybe something with hojicha, whatever that was.

"Which is your favorite?" she asked Lucy.

"Probably the strawberries and cream. Though the yuzu ginger is good, too. I think the dark chocolate raspberry is our most popular, or maybe the matcha and red bean."

That didn't make her decision any easier, but that was okay. Amy grinned.

At last, she decided on the matcha and red bean roll cake, as well as one of their fancy teas. Sencha. The prices nearly made her grimace—much more expensive than Tim Hortons—but she told herself it was okay.

Lucy said she'd bring everything over, so Amy tucked herself into the bench seating. Next to her, a man was typing on his laptop. On her other side, two women were having an animated conversation. She took out her book, but she didn't start reading. It was too exciting to be here in Toronto at last.

Her roll cake and tea arrived. The tea, which was already

steeped, was served not in a teapot or cup, but in a glass jug of sorts. She poured some tea into the little handle-less teacup, then had a bite of her cake.

The green cake was light and not too strong, and the cream inside, with a little red bean, was delicious. She'd never had anything sweet with beans before, and it wasn't chocolate, but it was still pretty good.

Next, she tried the tea. It was a bit grassy, though not unpleasant, and with a few more sips, she'd get used to it.

She took out her book and read for twenty minutes while she slowly savored her cake and drank her tea. She was currently reading the sixth Sierra Wu book by Megan Chen. It was an urban fantasy series set in San Francisco that she absolutely adored. The cover had an ominous background, and Sierra Wu was standing at the forefront, wearing jeans and a black tank top and looking totally kick-ass.

After leaving Harbord Coffee Bar, she arrived back at the house and stood outside for another minute, admiring it. She glanced at the house on the right, separated from hers by the narrowest of paths. An older woman named Paula lived there. Amy had met her when she'd visited the house a few months ago, but when she'd knocked on the door today, nobody had answered.

She had no idea who lived in the house attached to hers, though.

Someday soon, she'd make a point of introducing herself to her neighbors—or was that sort of thing not done in Toronto? Well, she'd do it anyway.

But for now, she'd have a pre-dinner drink on her patio.

Her backyard was tiny. Yards were never this tiny in Silver River, but space was at a premium in downtown Toronto. The small patio took up a good third of the yard. Aunt Frances had owned some decent patio furniture, which Amy had set out earlier.

She brought a glass of red wine outside, along with her book. She set everything down on the little table, and then she registered a noise coming from the yard to the left.

Her neighbor must be cutting the grass.

She bounded over to the low fence that separated their yards and stood there slack-jawed.

Holy fuck, her new neighbor was *hot*.

He was East Asian, maybe five or ten years older than her. His chest, back, and arms were covered in tattoos.

She knew this because he was shirtless. He wore only a pair of black gym shorts, slung low on his hips. His upper half was on full display. The sight of his arms was nearly enough to make her drool, but then she shifted her gaze to his pecs, and…oh my God. Those were gorgeous, too.

There were no men like this in Silver River.

His expression was serious, as though he was concentrating very hard on this activity. He reminded her of Sierra Wu's love interest, Rebel, though her imagination hadn't been able to conjure up something quite as hot as the man before her now.

Did he have a wife? If so, why wasn't she also having a drink and watching him?

Yes, this was certainly turning out to be a very good day.

Since the yards were small, it didn't take him long to finish his task. When he turned off the lawn mower, Amy waved and shouted, "Hey!"

He didn't seem to notice her, however, just put the lawn mower away with the same concentration he'd given to cutting the grass.

"Hey!" she said brightly with another wave as he headed toward the back door of his house. "I'm your new neighbor."

Finally, he turned in her direction, and she swallowed hard. He really was attractive.

But he didn't say anything. Didn't wave.

No, all he gave her was the slightest of nods before going inside.

Well, that was disappointing.

~

Later, Amy headed to Koreatown, since it was nearby on Bloor. She ventured into a store with cute notebooks, greeting cards, and BTS stuff. She came out with a little notebook and alpaca oven mitts.

After wandering around for a while, she went to a restaurant and ordered bibimbap. Several tiny appetizers came first, and she was about to protest and say she hadn't ordered them, but it looked like every table had the same dishes. She tried what looked like kimchi, then the bean sprouts. Both good.

Her bibimbap came in a stone bowl. There were several neat piles of different vegetables and meat around the edge of the bowl, with an egg in the center, all on top of rice. She took a picture for her new Instagram account, kicking herself for not taking a picture of her cake earlier, and looked up how to eat bibimbap. Apparently, she was supposed to mix it all up.

After dinner, she practically skipped back to the house, passing coffee shops and bars and restaurants. She counted three sushi restaurants in one block. How did they all survive?

The best part was that she had a whole month of this before she started school. Not that she wasn't excited about going back to school, but she hadn't had a break in a long time.

If she'd tried to take a staycation in Silver River, it wouldn't have worked. Her parents and her brothers would always have something for her to do. She was the youngest of three, the only girl and the only one who wasn't married, and everyone assumed she was always free to do favors for them.

But now, Amy was far away. Plus, she was going to get better at saying *no*.

No, Mom, I will not drive you to North Bay.

No, Fred, I will not babysit the twins for six hours on Saturday. No, I will not babysit with no notice if there isn't an emergency.

No, Shane, I will not vacuum and do the dishes while you sit there and play videogames. No, I will not make your lunch. No, I will not plan every single date.

When she'd met Shane at a party, there had been an immediate attraction. They'd slept together and somehow fallen into a relationship. She was so pleased to have a boyfriend for the first time in years that she hadn't minded doing all the work in the relationship.

Shane had never done anything for her, and she'd felt like she should be grateful simply because he wanted her around.

But that was all wrong. She would not settle for that shit again.

Amy had *standards* now.

And after her experience with Shane, she wasn't looking to date anytime soon. Her neighbor was good-looking, but she quickly brushed that idea aside. Nope, now wasn't the time.

That night, as Amy tried to fall asleep in her new room, instead of thinking of bibimbap or roll cakes, she thought of her neighbor. Although Rebel was usually getting in fights or stealthily spying on bad guys, she kept picturing her neighbor doing the sexy activity of...cutting the grass. Without a shirt.

She tried to stretch her imagination and only came up with him sitting on a riding lawn mower or pulling out weeds.

Also without a shirt, of course.

~

I am a confident woman.

I do not let people take advantage of me.

Amy had decided what to write in her new notebook: positive affirmations.

On the cover of the notebook was an illustration of a fluffy white puppy, a red cherry on its head. It was sitting on an ice cream cone. Amy hadn't been able to help herself from buying it yesterday, even though she had no idea what to do with it.

But she'd figured it out this morning over Cheerios and lots of coffee. She'd struggled to sleep last night thanks to her excitement and the unfamiliar noise of the city.

I will make friends in Toronto.

I love myself.

I am beautiful and...

Her phone beeped, and Amy nearly spilled her coffee.

Ooh, it was someone replying to the ad she'd posted for a roommate, just an hour ago.

Aunt Frances's—Amy's—house was more than big enough for one person, and the income from renting out a room would help pay the bills and property tax. She probably could have advertised for two or three roommates, given the size of the house, but she'd thought one would be enough. She'd looked at several ads the other day and determined a reasonable cost for a room in a shared house. Vacancies in Toronto weren't high, and the location was great, so she'd figured it wouldn't take long to find a roommate.

But an hour? She hadn't expected that.

She checked the e-mail to see who her potential roommate was. Would it be a man or a woman? A fellow grad student, perhaps? That could be fun.

She stilled when she saw the person's name.

Sierra Wu.

And she wanted to move in *today*.

[2]

OF COURSE, Amy knew that Sierra Wu wouldn't show up in tight jeans and a tight tank top, brandishing a sword and fighting off demons.

She *knew* that.

But her new roommate had the same name as her favorite fictional character. What were the odds? They were definitely going to be best friends.

Slow down, Amy.

This whole thing was not going slowly, though. Her potential roommate had contacted her three hours ago by email. They hadn't even talked on the phone, and now it was one o'clock, and she was supposed to be here any minute.

Sierra had told Amy that her plans had fallen through at the last minute. She had to be out of her old apartment today, but she had nowhere to go, and the movers were coming soon, and she would be ever so grateful.

Amy had said yes.

She sat on a chair on her tiny front porch—there was only room for one chair—and waited for Sierra to arrive.

At precisely one o'clock, a slight Asian woman in jeans, a blue T-shirt, and a bouncy ponytail approached the house.

Amy jumped up. "You must be Sierra!" she said, careful to sound enthusiastic, but not *too* enthusiastic. "I'm Amy."

She held out her hand, and Sierra shook it.

"Nice to meet you. Roomie," Sierra added with a smile.

She looked like she was no older than twenty-five.

"You're an engineer?" Sierra asked, nodding at the iron ring on Amy's hand.

"Yep," Amy said. "Civil engineer. I'm going back to school to do my master's."

"I have an engineering degree, too." Sierra's face clouded over. "Not that I use it."

"What do you do now?"

"I own a greeting card shop in Baldwin Village."

"That's so cool," Amy said, though she had no idea where Baldwin Village was. "Where did you go to school?"

"Queen's."

"Me, too!"

See? Toronto wasn't really that big after all.

"What year?" Amy asked.

It turned out that Amy had finished two years after Sierra, which was surprising—Sierra was clearly older than she looked. They discussed a couple of profs, Sierra handed over a check for first and last month's rent, and then the small moving truck showed up.

"I have a good amount of stuff," Sierra said. "I'm used to living alone. Ever since…Well, anyway." She shook her head. "I'm sure you have furniture of your own, so if we don't need it all and it doesn't fit in the basement, I'll arrange to put it in storage."

"What happened to the place you were going to move to?"

"It burned down last night."

"It…burned down?"

"Yup. Small apartment building, whole thing went up in

flames. No one was seriously injured, fortunately, but it left me without a place to live. I mean, my parents would be willing to have me back, but…" Sierra shuddered. "Not happening."

"Oh, I understand. I'm not living with my parents again, either."

"So, thank you. For letting me move in today."

It took over an hour for the men, who were nowhere near as attractive as the Rebel look-alike next door, to move everything in. It was a little tough in the narrow house with steep staircases, but they managed. Sierra did have lots of stuff, but luckily, Amy had a decent-sized house. She'd been planning to turn the second-floor room facing the street into a reading room of sorts. It had a bay window, and she'd always imagined curling up by a bay window and reading. Sierra had furniture for the room, which was awesome.

While Sierra unpacked her things, Amy made a quick trip to the coffee bar to get some treats. There were so many exciting places to try that it seemed silly to return to the place she'd been yesterday, but she knew their food was good.

"Hey," Amy said to Lucy, who was working again today. "I'll have the dark chocolate raspberry and yuzu ginger roll cakes. To go this time, please."

When she got back to the house, she made a pot of coffee and a pot of tea, not knowing which Sierra would prefer, then invited her new roommate down.

Sierra chose the coffee; Amy went for the tea so it wouldn't go to waste.

"Which would you like?" Amy gestured to the roll cakes.

"Oh my God, are those from Harbord Coffee Bar?"

"They are."

"The yuzu ginger is my favorite, but…"

Amy must have looked slightly disappointed, even though she'd tried not to show it. She'd been curious about that cake.

"We'll split them both," Sierra declared.

Amy got a knife and cut them in half.

"So, I have to ask you," Sierra said. "This is your house, correct?"

"Yep."

"You own a house, and you're a student. I don't mean to pry, but—"

"My eighty-five-year-old great aunt died and left it to me."

Aunt Frances had never married and had no children of her own. She'd left a small amount of money to Amy's brothers and cousins, but Amy had gotten the house. There had been a note saying it was to thank Amy for looking after her grandmother, Frances's older sister, in the last years of her life.

"You inherited a whole-ass house?" Sierra asked. "I mean, I'm sorry for your loss."

Heh. She talked a little like the fictional Sierra Wu.

"It's okay. I didn't know her well. But she gave me the perfect opportunity to move to Toronto."

"Where did you live before?"

"Silver River. It's a small town north of Sudbury."

Sierra chocked on her yuzu ginger cake. "*North* of Sudbury? How long of a drive is it?"

"About four and a half hours."

"How many people live there?"

"Two thousand."

Sierra looked horrified. She didn't say this, of course, and she quickly schooled her expression to something neutral.

"It's fine," Amy said. "I'm not insulted. I lived there my whole life, except when I was away at school, but I was itching to get out."

"I called Kingston a small town when I was at university."

"Kingston? It's a proper city. Over a hundred thousand people."

"Yeah, my friend Charlotte laughed at me. She's from a small town, too. But living in a place smaller than Kingston? I can't imagine it. Where did you eat?"

"There's a Tim Hortons, a pizza place, and a diner. You have to go into Sudbury if you want more than that. But last night, I saw three sushi restaurants in a block!"

"There's a stretch on Queen with four ramen restaurants in half a block."

"Ooh, I've never had ramen before. Other than the instant stuff."

"You want to go tonight?" Sierra asked. "I closed the store for the day because of the move, and I want to enjoy my day off. Unpacking?" She made a dismissive gesture. "That can wait."

Amy tried not to show her excitement. She was becoming friends with her roommate, and someone else was making plans for once. How cool was that?

The ramen restaurant was pretty great. She got something called black tonkotsu ramen, which had black garlic oil, and the broth was so rich and tasty. She also got karaage because it was only two bucks if you ordered ramen. The small pieces of fried chicken were delicious.

"I have a question for you," she said when they were halfway done their ramen.

"Yes?" Sierra seemed slightly wary now.

"Did you know that you have the same name as..." Amy trailed off when Sierra rolled her eyes.

Oh, no! Had she offended her new roommate?

"The urban fantasy series by Megan Chen. Yes, I'm aware. It's hard to miss. Every other person who meets me mentions it. Are you a big fan? Is that why you wanted to live with me?"

"I *am* a big fan. I own all the books. But you were the first one to reply." Amy shrugged. She didn't want to make a big deal of this now.

"It's almost as bad as being named Harry Potter. Or Bridget Jones. Or Alice in Wonderland."

Amy snorted and spilled some of her broth. "I can imagine." The series had become massively popular since the first book was published seven years ago.

"I used to like my name. It wasn't too common—I've never met another Sierra in real life. But now, I feel like I should spend my time slaying demons."

"I'm sure you could. If you wanted to."

Sierra laughed. "I did read the first book, but I found the main character's name kind of distracting." She smiled at Amy.

Okay. They were going to be fine. But real-life Sierra Wu was understandably a bit awkward about sharing her name with fictional Sierra Wu. Amy wouldn't bring it up again.

When they got back to the house, Amy turned to Sierra and said, "I've got a bottle of red wine I opened yesterday. You want to have some on the back patio?"

"Absolutely," Sierra said. "Just let me get changed first."

Amy brought two glasses and the bottle of wine out to the backyard, her heart beating a little quickly. The last time she'd been here, she'd seen a hot tattooed guy cutting the grass.

Of course, he wouldn't be doing that today. Sadly, grass didn't grow that fast.

Amy rather hoped it rained a lot so the grass would grow quickly, but that wouldn't be good for wandering the city, though she did have a cute ladybug umbrella that she'd bought online. She didn't care if it was childish. It was *awesome*. She had yet to use it, though. In Silver River, she'd been afraid someone—likely a relative—would see it and think it was stupid.

Once she'd set down the wine, she glanced at the backyard on the left, and her skin prickled when she saw him. He was reclining in a lounge chair, a drink in his hand.

He wasn't shirtless today, but she could still see some of his tattoos. And muscles.

She skipped over to the fence, pleased she was wearing her blue dress with white polka dots and a red belt. She may have been thinking of him when she put it on before going out for ramen with Sierra.

"Hey!" she said.

Like last night, he gave her a slight nod.

Then he returned to brooding over his drink.

Hmph.

Amy stepped away from the fence, poured herself a glass of wine, and sat down. Sierra joined her, and for the next hour, as darkness fell and the lights of the city came on, they sat outside and talked.

But her gaze kept straying to the yard on the left.

Who was he? What was his story?

When would he cut the grass again?

"Auntie Amy!" Abigail shrieked.

"Hi, sweetie," Amy said.

This was the first time she'd had a video call with her six-year-old niece. She was used to living in the same town as her and seeing her every week.

"You look pretty," Abigail said.

"Why, thank you. But shouldn't you be in bed now?"

It was nine thirty at night, and Sierra had just gone to her room after their wine. Amy was in her own room, doing some organizing.

"I couldn't sleep," Abigail said. "So I stole Daddy's phone and called you."

"Does your dad know?"

"Nope! I just really wanted to sing you a song. I learned it yesterday."

Abigail loved singing. For a six-year-old, she had a decent voice. Unfortunately, her musical choices were, well, those of a six-year-old.

"It's a Christmas song," Abigail said. "Are you ready?"

"I'm ready."

"Jingle bells, Batman smells!" Abigail began at the top of her lungs, more off-tune than usual. "Robin laid—"

Abigail's face suddenly disappeared, and there was a bit of a commotion before Amy's brother, Fred, appeared onscreen.

"Sorry," he said, "She's supposed to be in bed."

"Daddy!" Abigail cried. "Let me finish my song."

"You can call Aunt Amy back tomorrow, okay? It was a very fine performance. A very highbrow choice."

"Are you making fun of me?" It sounded like a little girl was stomping her foot on the other end of the call.

"Go to bed, sweetheart." Fred turned back to Amy. "How's the big bad city?"

"It's great!" she said.

He ran a hand over his face. "I still can't believe you moved to Toronto."

"Well, I always wanted to do it, and I finally had the chance."

"Abigail misses you. So do the twins."

Yes, here it was. The guilt trip. "I've only been gone a couple days."

"But you're not coming back until Thanksgiving, right?"

"That's the plan. I don't have a car, so I'll only come back when I rent one."

A car had been a necessity in her old life, but she hadn't wanted the hassle—and expense—of one in Toronto. There was a laneway out back, and she had the world's tiniest garage, which was better than street parking, but still. She was also, frankly, terrified of driving in Toronto. So much traffic. Better to walk and take the subway everywhere, especially since she was only a six-minute walk from the subway station.

"I don't understand why you need to do this," Fred said. "You had a life and a job here. Who's going to look after the kids and cook dinner when we go curling on Thursday nights?"

"You can hire Janey."

"She's not as good at putting them to bed as you are."

And he'd have to pay her, whereas Amy would babysit for free.

She decided to change the topic. "I already got a roommate. She moved in today."

"How well do you know her?"

"I met her when she moved in, but she's awesome."

"You think everyone's awesome," Fred muttered. "Next thing you know, you'll be murdered in your sleep."

"Daddy, what's murdered?" said a little voice.

One of the twins must be up, which meant the other wasn't far behind.

Fred ended the call, and Amy slumped on her bed.

Her family had made it seem as if she was abandoning them by moving to Toronto. But she was a thirty-year-old woman. She deserved to have her own life, right? It wasn't like she wouldn't talk to them every week and visit them on holidays. She was still part of their lives, but she'd always been there at a moment's notice, and now…she wasn't. And while Fred wasn't upset that she'd inherited more than he had, her other brother, Steven, was resentful.

Amy was a people pleaser, and it was hard to accept that no one in her family was happy with this move. And she would miss her nieces, it was true.

There was a sudden ache in her heart.

She took out her puppy notebook and started writing.

I will not feel guilty for living where I want.

I will build a great life for myself in Toronto.

I will get my neighbor to talk to me and maybe take off his shirt when he's not cutting the grass…

Whoa. She should probably rein in her fantasies. After all, he'd yet to say a single word to her. She bet he had a sexy voice, though.

Stop it, Amy!

She turned out the lights at eleven o'clock, but like Abigail, she couldn't sleep.

Was moving here the right decision? And would the man next door ever talk to her?

Well, she had an idea for the weekend…

[3]

Victor Choi's new neighbors were pissing him off.

The house attached to his had sat empty for many months, ever since Frances Oliynyk had passed away last winter after a short illness. Frances had lived in that house for decades, much longer than he'd been here. He'd cut her grass in the summer and shoveled her walkway in the winter, and they'd shared brief conversations about the weather, but little more. That was the way they'd both liked it. Limited social interaction.

Frances had been a quiet neighbor, but now, things were different.

There appeared to be two young women living next to him. They'd been out chatting on the patio the last two evenings, which they were perfectly entitled to do, of course.

But he missed his peace and quiet.

One of his new neighbors was a petite Asian woman. He hadn't had a close look at her. The other woman…

Well.

She was the one who really bothered him.

She was white. Blonde hair and brown eyes and an irritatingly perky demeanor that made him think of Meg Ryan in *You've Got Mail.*

Yes, he'd seen that movie, against his better judgment, back in the days when he'd dated.

Quite a while ago now.

Anyway, this neighbor, she reminded him a bit of Meg Ryan with long hair. But sexier.

She had big breasts, a thick waist, and ample hips, and she was always wearing these goddamn dresses. The first day, it had been a sunflower dress. The next day, a polka dot dress, which was his favorite so far. Yesterday, a more casual green dress. He suspected she knew exactly how cute she looked.

She also kept smiling and laughing.

God, it was horrid.

It was her laugh, more than anything, that bugged him. Her laugh was loud and intrusive, and she seemed to laugh a lot when talking to the other woman. He'd had to go inside last night because it was bothering him too much.

To his horror, she'd even tried to introduce herself, though when he'd only given her a brief nod, she hadn't bothered telling him her name.

Paula, when she'd cornered him the other day while walking her obnoxious puppy, had said that Frances's grandniece had inherited the house. Since Victor hadn't seen a "for sale" sign, he assumed this woman with the cute dresses was the grandniece, and she'd decided to live here.

He couldn't blame her. These were nice Victorians, and Frances had kept hers in good condition. Besides, you couldn't beat the location. That was why his brother…

Victor shook his head and tried to think of other things.

But that reminded him: he needed to water his brother's cacti. He went up to the small sunroom on the second floor, and he'd just finished watering the last cactus—the extra-spiky one was his favorite—when the doorbell rang.

For fuck's sake. Probably a salesman.

He ignored it, but then it rang again. He stomped downstairs, flung open the door, and was promptly rendered speechless.

It was her again.

He'd already nodded at her twice. What more did she want from him? Was she going to ring his doorbell every Saturday?

What a nightmare. Ten in the morning was far too early for this shit.

But damn, she looked good. She was wearing a red dress with white polka dots. How many polka dot dresses did she have?

He particularly liked this one. It gave him a great view of her cleavage, not that he was looking. Of course not.

There was a white bow in her hair, and when he looked down, he noted her white sandals and red toenails. Why was she so fucking color-coordinated?

"Hello," he said gruffly.

"Hi!" That damn perky voice again. "I'm Amy." She stuck out her hand.

Since he didn't see any way out of this, he shook it. "Victor."

"I guess we share a wall now, Victor!" She laughed that annoying laugh of hers. "Where I'm from, there are no semi-detached houses, but Toronto is different."

He did not ask where she was from; he was not keen on continuing this conversation. He supposed it was good to actually meet his new neighbor and learn her name, but now that was over and she could go away.

"Have you lived here long?" she asked. "The elderly lady who used to live next door was my great aunt. Did you know her?"

"Mm."

"Anyway, I'm here in Toronto for school! Always wanted to do my master's. But I'm not starting until September, so I have lots of free time until then."

Dear God. She'd probably get on his every last nerve.

But certain parts of him were thrilled with the idea of her parading around the backyard in a series of dresses.

"What are you studying?"

Why had he asked her a question? What was wrong with him? He wanted to get this conversation over with, didn't he?

"Structural engineering," she said. "I'm doing an MASc. I won't bother you with the details of my project."

He grunted as his gaze drifted over her body again. This time, he noticed something in her hand. A Tupperware of cookies from the looks of it?

His mouth watered, much to his annoyance. A new neighbor who'd go so far as to bring him cookies was not what he wanted.

She saw where he was looking. "I made you chocolate chip cookies. My grandmother's recipe. They're really good, trust me." She lifted up the lid.

They smelled amazing. Freshly baked.

Okay, he wasn't annoyed anymore, and he was thinking of her walking around the kitchen in a cute apron—he bet she had a cute apron—and…

He cut off that train of thought.

"Thank you," he said.

"Just put the container back on my porch when you're finished. You don't have to ring the doorbell—I can tell you're not big on socializing."

Well, geez. What could have possibly given her that impression?

His lips twitched, amused at her boldness.

"If you need anything, just, um, let me know." He should be kind. After all, she was being very kind, even if it wasn't really his thing.

"Don't worry, I will!"

That sounded ominous.

She skipped down his steps, off to frolic with unicorns or whatever the fuck she did.

He brought the container of cookies into the kitchen and looked at it suspiciously. Had she baked pixie dust into them?

He picked one up and had a bite. Nothing bad happened.

No, only good things happened, because the cookies, as she'd promised, were delicious and contained a generous amount of chocolate chips, which was how he liked them. They were still slightly warm, and he had to stop himself from moaning.

Over a goddamn cookie.

But although she baked great cookies and looked good in polka dots, he couldn't help hoping that their interactions would be kept to a minimum.

He liked his privacy.

That morning, Amy had baked three dozen of the best chocolate chip cookies in the world, one dozen for each of her neighbors—to make a good impression—and the others to keep for her and Sierra.

First, she'd gone to visit her neighbor on the left. Lawn Mower Dude, aka Rebel.

No, *Victor*. She knew his name now.

She'd worn her favorite dress, not for any particular reason of course, and she thought he'd been checking her out, but perhaps that was her imagination.

It had been hard to focus in his presence, since he was even hotter up close.

The hard lines of his face, his cropped hair, his intense dark eyes…

And when he'd taken the container of cookies from her, she hadn't been able to stop staring at his forearms.

She'd been a touch nervous, so she'd babbled a bit, and he hadn't helped—he'd said very little and hadn't exactly been friendly.

Which shouldn't surprise her, after their earlier encounters.

But he hadn't told her to get off his property, and he'd thanked her and even asked her a question. Without much enthusiasm, but still.

She'd win him over eventually.

Once he'd tasted her delicious cookies, he should already be halfway there.

She hadn't seen any evidence that he lived with someone else —she'd peeked into his front hall, and there were no shoes that would suggest another occupant—but she couldn't be a hundred percent sure.

Oh, well.

For now, she'd focus on her other neighbor, Paula.

But when she knocked on the door, it wasn't Paula who answered. It was a different woman, maybe sixty-five, with short white hair, glasses, and an elegant purple scarf.

"Hi. I'm Amy, your new next-door neighbor. Are you new to the neighborhood, too? I saw another woman when I was here before—"

A white ball of fluff shot out of nowhere and barked excitedly around her ankles.

"Beast!" said the woman. "Get back inside."

"Oh, I don't mind." Amy knelt down. "Can I pet him?"

The woman nodded, and Amy ran her hand over the pup and scratched behind his ears. He yipped excitedly.

"His name is Beast?" Amy said.

The dog barked again, wagging his tail.

"*Her* name is Beast."

Beast was adorable and had the presence of a dog four times her size.

"I'm Debbie," the other woman said. "The person you met before…"

A familiar woman walked to the door and set her hand on

Debbie's shoulder. She had long gray hair and was shorter than Debbie.

"Nice to see you again, Amy," Paula said. "You've met my partner, Debbie?"

It had been foolish of Amy to think that Paula must have moved, just because another woman had answered the door. Of course two women in their sixties could live together.

"I brought you homemade cookies." Amy held out the container.

Beast barked again.

"No, not for you, I'm sorry," she said.

"Thank you." Paula took the container from her. "Although I think it should work the other way around. We should be the ones baking you cookies to welcome you to the neighborhood."

"It's no trouble at all. I like baking."

"How are you finding Toronto? I assume this is quite the change from your hometown."

"It is, but I love it."

Yep, everything was going swimmingly, aside from the fact that her family was guilt-tripping her and the man next door wasn't friendly. Paula and Debbie seemed nice, though.

"Have you met Victor?" Paula asked. "He lives on the other side of you."

"Yes! I was just over at his place."

Paula and Debbie exchanged a look.

Was it something in Amy's expression? Was she turning pink?

"He was rather…gruff," Amy said.

Beast barked in agreement.

"Yeah, he keeps to himself," Paula said, "but he's a good neighbor. Helped us repair our garage a couple summers ago."

"Does anyone else live there with him?" Amy asked.

"It's just Victor." Debbie exchanged another look with Paula. "I know it doesn't seem like the sort of place where a bachelor would live, but…" She shrugged.

Amy tried not to be excited upon learning it was just him.

She was determined to win him over. As a *friend*. Her love life was not her priority right now, and although Victor was completely different from Shane temperament-wise, she feared he would also take a lot and give nothing in return.

It wasn't like he'd shown interest in her anyway, though he seemed to have noticed her spectacular cleavage in this dress—but that was, admittedly, hard to miss.

Besides, he was too grouchy. She didn't need a man bringing her down, no matter how good-looking he was, no matter how much she wanted to trace her finger over every inch of his chest. Although maybe he'd be different if she was touching him…

Her hand flew to her lips.

"Nice to meet you, Debbie!" she chirped. "Good to see you again, Paula. I'll get out of your hair now. Bye, Beast." She petted her fluffy friend once more before heading down the steps.

Too bad Victor didn't have a dog—at least, she hadn't seen any sign of one. That would give them something to bond over.

But she *would* succeed at Project Victor, aka Project Make-My-Neighbor-Like-Me. Amy couldn't stand to not be friendly with her neighbor.

She walked through her front door and helped herself to one of her cookies. She was about to reach for a second one when her phone buzzed.

Do you have any plans tonight? Sierra asked.

[4]

AMY WAS MEETING Sierra's friends from university, and she was a bundle of nerves.

Three new women. Three potential friends.

Apparently, Sierra and her friends met a couple times a month at Ossington Cider Bar. Amy had never been to a bar dedicated to cider before. She'd had Strongbow, but that was it.

She'd convinced Sierra to walk there. It was about a half-hour walk, and it was a lovely night. They headed down College Street, through Little Italy, and Amy tried not to be distracted by all the shops and restaurants.

She was still wearing her red dress with white polka dots, which hopefully didn't look too worse for wear, since she'd been wearing it all day.

When they arrived, it was just before eight, and none of Sierra's friends were there yet. They managed to snag a table in the small backyard patio, which Amy thought was adorable. There were potted plants around the edge and fairy lights twinkled above them.

Eight ciders were on tap. This place made their own cider—

how neat was that? They had another location farther north in the city.

Amy decided to have a flight of four ciders so she could try as many as possible.

When the waiter, an attractive white man with a beard, came around, she ordered strawberry Earl Grey—she'd never heard of tea in cider before—blood orange, cranberry, and a cider that had been aged in whiskey barrels. Sierra ordered a glass of the strawberry Earl Grey.

"We should get some food, too." Amy picked up the food menu after the waiter had left. "Since we haven't eaten dinner."

"The fried chicken is really good."

"We'll get some of that, then."

"As are the Brussels sprouts."

Amy raised her eyebrows. "Um…"

Good was not a word she'd use to describe Brussels sprouts.

"Trust me," Sierra said. "They're caramelized, and there's lots of bacon and cheese. If you don't like them, I'll eat them all and you can order something else."

Amy was still doubtful, but also a little intrigued.

"Is Sierra trying to convince you to order the Brussels sprouts?" a woman asked as she sat down across from them. She was wearing an elegant black shirt with a silver necklace. Her dark brown hair was partially pulled back, and her lips were painted pink.

"She is," Amy said with a laugh.

"Don't let her. She thinks those things are fucking orgasmic, but at the end of the day, they're just bitter vegetables with bacon to hide some of the taste."

"Well, if Sierra thinks they're orgasmic," Amy said, feeling slightly weird about using that word, "then I have to try them."

The server came around to take their orders. Sierra ordered their food, and her friend ordered a burger and a glass of blackberry nectarine cider.

"Our server is hot," the woman said as he walked away. "Don't think I've seen him here before." She stared at him for a moment, then looked at Amy. "I'm Nicole."

"I'm Amy."

"You did engineering at Queen's, too?"

"Yup. Civil."

"I was in engineering physics, but then I did a graduate degree in financial math."

"Nicole works in finance now," Sierra said. "On Bay Street."

"Oh, wow," Amy said.

An East Asian woman, dressed in jeans and a gray T-shirt, sat down next to Nicole.

"I'm Charlotte," she said. "You must be Amy."

"Yes, that's me!" Amy said, her voice sounding high and nervous to her ears.

Charlotte arched an eyebrow.

"Charlotte studied geological engineering," Sierra said. "She works from home as a geophysicist, and it's always an honor when she actually puts on pants and leaves her apartment to join us for an evening."

Charlotte snorted. "Hope they have something good on tap." She grabbed a menu. "The perry's good. Nice and dry. I bet Nicole ordered the blackberry nectarine."

"You know me so well," Nicole said.

The waiter returned and set a flight of ciders in front of Amy. Someone had written on the little wooden tray in chalk to identify which cider was which. He also set Sierra and Nicole's drinks in front of them, then took Charlotte's order.

Nicole sipped her cider. "Mmm. That's delicious." She passed it to Charlotte.

"That's fucking juice," Charlotte said after having a taste. "Why order cider when you want to drink juice?"

"Charlotte prefers hers dry," Sierra explained. "They always do this."

"Juice doesn't have alcohol," Nicole said. "Unlike *this*. Cheers." She held up her glass, and Sierra clinked hers with Nicole's. Amy grabbed one of her samples and joined in.

She took a sip. This was the blood orange cider, and it was, to her surprise, not orange-colored. In fact, it was quite pale, and not overly sweet. But not too dry, either, and very orangey.

"Hey. I'm Rose."

Amy startled. She hadn't noticed the woman sit down beside her.

Rose was soft-spoken. She wasn't petite like Sierra and Charlotte, but closer to Amy's size. She had glasses and a nice smile, and she wore a fluttery dress and a few necklaces.

"I love your dress," Amy said.

"Thank you. I love yours, too, but I could never pull it off. It's too bold."

"Nonsense," Nicole said. "You totally could." She leaned away from the table and nodded at the server, who came over and took Rose's order. Strawberry Earl Grey cider.

A good choice. Amy had tried all of her ciders by now, and that was her favorite.

"Rose is the only one who actually works as an engineer," Sierra said.

Rose nodded. "I'm an electrical engineer."

"If you went to Queen's," Nicole said, "you may have noticed that it was pretty white. The four of us"—she gestured around the table—"are more than half of the Asian women in engineering in our year, out of six hundred or so students. I'm part Asian— sometimes I tell people that before they ask awkward questions. Given where I grew up in Toronto, the whiteness of Queen's was rather shocking to me."

"I'm from a small town," Charlotte said. "There was an Asian family next door for part of my childhood, but that was all. It was very white."

Nicole turned to Amy. "I hear you inherited a house."

"Yes. I'm lucky."

"I'm glad you were able to give Sierra a place to live."

"Me, too," Charlotte said. "Otherwise she might have asked to stay with me temporarily, and I don't like living with people."

"You might have had to put on pants," Sierra said. "What a shame."

"You don't appreciate my struggles," Charlotte muttered.

When the rest of the drinks and food arrived, Amy eyed the Brussels sprouts suspiciously.

Sierra popped one in her mouth and made an exaggerated groan. "So good."

Amy tried one next. The caramelization, bacon, and cheese mostly covered up the Brussels sprout-ness. She could still detect some bitterness, but it worked with everything else.

"So, are you a convert?" Nicole asked before having a bite of her burger.

"I think I am. As long as they're smothered in bacon and cheese…yep, I approve."

Rose chuckled softly beside her, and Amy's heart warmed.

She wanted to make people laugh. She wanted these women to like her.

She hadn't had a group of friends to hang out with in Silver River. Many of her high school friends had left the area.

"I don't like Brussels sprouts at all," Nicole said, "no matter how much bacon there is."

"You prefer eggplant," Charlotte deadpanned. "Long, thick eggplant."

Nicole snorted while drinking her cider.

"Please behave," Sierra said with faux sternness. "Amy only just met you all, and she's my roommate."

Nicole ignored her and looked around the patio. When the server came out the back door, she flipped her hair over her shoulder and winked at him. He nearly stumbled with a tray full of cider but managed to straighten himself just in time.

"It's been a while," Nicole said. "I mean, not really a long time, but unlike Sierra, I can't depend on Brussels sprouts to give me orgasms. Do you have a boyfriend or girlfriend, Amy? A friend with benefits? Anything along those lines?"

Amy couldn't help thinking of Victor next door, but nothing would happen with him.

"No," she said.

"It took you a long time to respond," Sierra remarked.

"Well, we do have a really hot neighbor."

"Excuse me? You didn't tell me this. Which side?"

"The one we share a wall with. The first night I was in the house, I saw him in the backyard without a shirt. He was very tattooed and muscled."

Four women stared at Amy, mouths hanging open.

Nicole picked up her phone. "What's your address? I'm coming over tomorrow."

Sierra shook her head. "Nope, I need to see this man first. See if he's drool-worthy."

"You didn't notice him sitting outside the other night," Amy said, "when we were drinking wine?"

"Apparently not."

"He doesn't seem to like me, though. Or maybe it's more that he doesn't like people in general, I don't know."

"I can relate," Charlotte said.

"I brought him a dozen cookies today," Amy said.

"A dozen?" Sierra turned to her. "There were only six for me."

"I also gave a dozen cookies to the women next door. Being neighborly, you know."

"Sure, sure." Nicole spun her glass on her coaster.

"Really! I just wanted to be friendly. I'm not looking to date right now."

"Mm-hmm."

"Are any of you married? Boyfriends or girlfriends?"

"Nah, we're all single," Nicole said. "Four single thirty-two-year-old women, free to hang out together and drink cider on Saturday nights. But..." She glanced at Sierra.

"I was briefly married," Sierra said. "Divorced now."

Amy tried not to look surprised.

"Don't worry, it didn't scar me for life," her new roommate went on. "He's a nice enough guy. We're still friends, sort of. Charlotte never got married, but she was nearly engaged."

"Yeah." Charlotte made a face. "Then he proposed at a fucking baseball game. I like baseball, but I absolutely hate public proposals." She shuddered. "My worst nightmare. Thousands of people staring at me, waiting for me to say yes? Just shoot me now."

"Shouldn't he have known you wouldn't like it?" Amy asked.

"Exactly. He should have known better. After all, we'd been together for three fucking years." She held up her glass and downed half her drink.

Amy finally tried the fried chicken thighs. They were delicious, though not as revolutionary as the Brussels sprouts.

"I don't date," Nicole said. "I just sleep with the men I find attractive." She tilted her head in the direction of the waiter.

"Nicole is all about one-night stands," Sierra explained.

"What about you?" Amy asked Rose.

"One day." She smiled at her glass.

"I need another drink," Nicole said. "Maybe more of that blackberry nectarine cider. Just to make Charlotte squirm."

"I'll also get the blackberry nectarine." Amy had nearly finished her flight.

"You're as bad as Nicole," Charlotte muttered. "Cider should be *dry*." But she shot Amy a smile.

They stayed on the patio for a few hours, chatting and drinking cider.

Just before midnight, they all headed out. Except for Nicole, who moved to a seat at the bar and ramped up her flirting with the waiter.

Amy was a little drunk, but that wasn't the main reason she

felt happy. She'd only been in Toronto for a week, and she'd just spent a night out with a few other women, surrounded by a light breeze, twinkling lights, and laughter. Everyone had been so nice to her.

"Thanks for inviting me," she said to Sierra as they stumbled out of their Uber.

As Amy searched for her keys in her purse, she glanced at the house next door. There were no lights on.

Was Victor out back, brooding in the dark? Or had he gone out for the evening? Or was he already in bed, perhaps with a bedmate?

Amy's pulse quickened as she hopped up the steps to her porch.

The Tupperware she'd given him was by the door. No note.

Victor was sitting in his backyard with a glass of scotch on the rocks and a few chocolate chip cookies. They really were delicious.

Normally, he would have gone to bed by now, but he didn't feel like sleeping and was positive he'd end up tossing and turning if he tried.

No ruckus from his new neighbors today. Amy seemed like the kind of person who'd go out on a Saturday night, so that wasn't surprising.

Victor, on the other hand, was decidedly not the kind of person who went out on a Saturday night. Or any night, really. Though his cousin was determined to add some "fun" to Victor's life and had texted him earlier, trying to convince him to go to a club.

What a nightmarish way to spend a night. A crowded dance floor? No, thank you.

Victor sipped his scotch and, to his irritation, wondered again what his neighbor had been up to tonight. Had she met a new man, seduced him with cookies, and giggled in his ear until he whisked her back to his place?

Victor clenched his glass, which made him even more irritated.

It didn't matter to him what she did. He liked his life of isolation.

It hadn't always been this way. He'd never been overly social, but once upon a time, he'd done more than go to the office and head right home afterward.

Best not to think of those days.

No, better to think of a certain woman in a polka dot dress instead.

[5]

IT WAS the one-week anniversary of the day Amy Sharpe had moved to Toronto. In that time, she'd walked thirty-five kilometers around the city and eaten bibimbap, ramen, Brussels sprouts, fried chicken, and lots of other amazing food. She'd tried bubble tea and five types of cider. She'd gotten a roommate and met her neighbors. She'd started making friends.

Amy still wasn't sleeping all that well—even though she lived on a residential street, there was more noise here than in Silver River—but last night, she'd had her best sleep yet.

This morning, after having some coffee and finishing the latest Sierra Wu book, she wasn't in the greatest mood. The book had ended on a cliffhanger, and she'd have to wait another eight months for the next one.

Well, at least she had lots of things to distract herself today.

Amy put on some shorts and a T-shirt, slathered herself in sunscreen, and headed outside. She planned to go for a leisurely walk, ending at Sierra's shop in Baldwin Village. She couldn't wait to see more of the city. It was all new and exciting.

First, she headed south to Kensington Market. It was busy, with cars inching ahead among all the pedestrians. There were breweries and coffee shops. Small stores selling cheese, spices, empanadas, and other wonderful things. After much debate, she bought an empanada, figuring it was small enough that she'd still have room for dumplings later.

There were many dessert options, too. An ice cream cone covered in gold foil—presumably that was mostly for Instagram? A bakery that only made donuts, with flavors she'd never seen at Tim Hortons. Lavender blueberry donuts tempted her, as did the chocolate cherry ones. Would the pineapple cake donuts be similar to her mother's amazing pineapple upside-down cake?

But Amy would not have dessert now. Sierra had said they'd go out for ice cream in Baldwin Village, and Amy didn't need donuts in addition to ice cream.

Most of the shops and restaurants were quite small, and some appeared to be in converted houses. There were a variety of murals. A colorful car with plants growing out of it.

Amy spent a while wandering around the vibrant market, then went to the dumpling shop in Chinatown that Sierra had recommended. XLB served one thing: xiaolongbao, or soup dumplings. Apparently this wasn't soup with dumplings, but dumplings with soup inside. Though she wasn't sure how that worked, she did love dumplings.

She ordered six dumplings and sat at the counter in the cramped shop. She didn't think she could manage to do this with chopsticks, so she used a spoon instead.

Amy burned her mouth on the first dumpling, then waited a few minutes before she attempted the second. The juicy filling exploded in her mouth, and she moaned in bliss. She dipped her third dumpling in a tiny amount of soy sauce and vinegar.

When she emerged from XLB, she was full, but not so full that she wouldn't be able to have ice cream soon. She passed grocers on Spadina selling a myriad of vegetables and fruit. Some she could identify; some she could not. Little old ladies with carts talked quickly in a language she couldn't understand. The signs were in Chinese and English.

She passed a souvenir shop with shot glasses and postcards that looked like they were from the last century. Bakeries selling all sorts of goodies she wouldn't try today, but she'd be back soon.

Cooked pigs hung from the ceiling in one of the restaurants she walked by. Another advertised all-day dim sum. Still another had hot pot—what exactly was that? She wanted to try it all. In Silver River, there had been no new foods and restaurants to try, and she'd gotten sick of her own cooking.

She headed down Baldwin Street, surprised it was residential, but when she'd walked for a few minutes, a small cluster of restaurants and other businesses appeared.

Ah. This must be Baldwin Village.

This section of the street was quite short, and she soon found Sierra's shop, Moonbeam Messages. The sign was purple with white letters in a swooping font.

"Hi, Amy," Sierra said as she walked the two steps from the counter to the door.

The small store was crowded with all sorts of cards and other cute things. There was a page of adorable puppy stickers that looked a bit like Beast.

Amy wished she could bring her nieces here. Alas, Canada Post would have to do.

"Don't feel like you need to buy anything," Sierra said. "It's alright."

"But I want to," Amy said.

There was a series of elaborate pop-up cards, opened up so you could see what was inside. Amy loved the Ferris wheel one.

Next, she came to a rack labeled "Moonbeam Originals."

"Are these your designs?" she asked Sierra.

"Um."

Amy had never seen her housemate like this before. Sierra

wasn't usually shy and uncertain. True, Amy hadn't known her for long, but still.

"I design them and have them printed," Sierra said, looking away.

They were all delightful. Whimsical, even when the subjects didn't exactly inspire whimsy. Like the family of raccoons, their heads popping up from a garbage can. The blue text said, "Greetings from Toronto." Amy picked it up. She was about to compliment her housemate, then glanced at Sierra and figured it would make her uncomfortable. No, she'd just spend her money here instead.

In the end, she got the Ferris wheel card for Abigail, the raccoon card for one of the twins, and a llama card for the other. It said, "Miss you a llama."

Once her purchases were secured in a paper bag, she headed outside. Sierra flipped the sign to "Be Back in Ten," and they went to Ginger Scoops.

The inside was cheerful and pink, and there was even a rocking unicorn.

Amy already loved it.

There were so many flavors of ice cream that she'd never encountered before. Green tea. Black sesame. Taro. Strawberry lychee sorbet.

"Ooh, you should try the durian," Sierra said. "It's a type of fruit."

"Okay, I'll order that and the green tea."

"No, don't order it. Try a sample first."

The woman behind the counter—her nametag said "Chloe"—handed her a spoon with pale yellow ice cream.

"This is a fruit?" Amy said, wrinkling her nose. "It smells like gas."

"Yeah, it's a love or hate kind of thing."

Warily, Amy slid the spoon into her mouth.

But despite the funky smell, she didn't mind the taste. She couldn't describe it—there was a hint of caramel, but also onion?

"It's actually not too bad," she said. "At least as good as those Brussels sprouts."

Sierra put a hand to her chest. "Don't you dare say that about my bacon-and-cheese-smothered Brussels sprouts. They're better than durian."

Amy laughed. "I think I'll order something else, though."

She felt silly getting an ice cream for its purple color, but she ordered the taro anyway, as well as the green tea. Sierra chose black sesame and Hong Kong milk tea for her flavors.

They sat outside under an umbrella and licked their cones. Amy had been walking around in the heat all day and she was sweating, even after the air conditioning of Moonbeam Messages. The ice cream was just what she needed. Sweet and creamy and cooling.

"How long have you had the shop?" Amy gestured across the street.

"Two years," Sierra replied.

"Did you work as an engineer before that?"

"Unfortunately, yes." Sierra paused. "I really shouldn't have studied engineering, and I remember almost nothing of what I learned in those four years of school."

"So why did you do it?"

Sierra shrugged. "I didn't know what I wanted to do with my life, and I knew my parents would approve of engineering. Just sort of happened. They're disappointed in me now. Divorced and running a greeting card shop isn't exactly the definition of success."

"But your shop is awesome!" Amy said. "Have your parents been to it?"

"No."

"They're in Toronto, right?"

"Yeah, in Scarborough."

Amy wanted to ask more questions, but she suspected Sierra didn't want to talk about it. She enjoyed her green and purple ice cream instead, feeling almost guilty that she had a month of freedom before starting school in September.

While most people were at their jobs, she'd get to explore Toronto and eat ice cream. Even gold-coated ice cream if she wanted. She'd also get to read, accompanied by a cup of tea or glass of wine, in the backyard whenever she wanted.

That was exactly what she did later that afternoon. Amy usually read e-books, though she bought her Sierra Wu books in paperback. She brought her e-reader and some wine to the patio, and a few minutes later, a very exciting noise started up.

The whir of the lawn mower.

It didn't take long to cut the grass in Victor's backyard.

He wished he had more to do outside, but thanks to all the rain in the past few days, his garden didn't need watering.

He turned off the lawn mower and was about to put it in his tiny garage out back, but then he happened to glance at the yard next to his.

She was there.

In fact, Amy was standing right at the wooden fence that separated their properties.

And she was staring at him.

Her lips parted in an "O" as he walked toward her, holding her gaze. Yep, she'd been admiring him, all right.

When he got to the fence, he could see that she wasn't wearing one of her dresses today, but a T-shirt and a pair of jean shorts. She was holding a glass of wine.

He smirked. "Whatcha doing?"

Wow, this was weird. He was actually starting a conversation. It wasn't like him.

"I…um…"

She laughed, slightly nervously. He still found her laugh rather annoying, but it was cute to see her at a loss for words, unlike when she'd come to his door on Saturday.

But it didn't take her long to find those words. "I was just enjoying my wine! It's a nice day, isn't it? After all the rain we've had—I guess that's why you had to cut the grass again. I'll cut mine tomorrow. Today, I was wandering around Kensington Market and Chinatown. I ate an empanada and soup dumplings. Have you ever had them? I bet you have. Then I went to my friend's card store and bought presents for my nieces, and I had ice cream! My nieces would love the ice cream shop, if they ever…"

She seemed to realize she'd been babbling and snapped her mouth shut.

His lips twitched. "You're enjoying yourself in Toronto?"

Oh my God. He'd asked her another question. Call the press! What a rare event!

She grinned, looking especially pleased that he was conversing with her. So damn *perky*.

"Yes!" she said. "I love it here. There's so much to see and do. And eat. I've definitely been doing a lot of eating. I'm from a small town called Silver River. I doubt you've heard of it. It's pretty in the fall, sure, but there's not much to do there, not even…"

She trailed off again as her gaze slid down his chest.

"You have so many tattoos!" she exclaimed.

"Mm-hmm. Great powers of observation."

She seemed unaffected by his sarcasm. "I always wanted a tattoo."

He arched a brow. "Let me guess. A butterfly? A daisy?"

She giggled. "No. The Golden Gate Bridge."

Well, that hadn't been what he'd expected.

"You like San Francisco?" he asked.

"I've never been. One day. My favorite series is set there, plus I always loved the pictures of the red bridge in the clouds. I do quite like bridges, you know. Too bad Toronto doesn't have a river running through the middle with lots of nice bridges. Like Paris. I'm a structural engineer—I told you that, right? I'm taking a course on bridges this fall."

He imagined her as the keener student with a row of freshly-sharpened pencils. She'd stick her hand straight up in the air and ask lots of questions.

Against his wishes, his lips twitched again.

"I'd get it here." Amy turned around and spread her hand over the back of her shoulder. "What do you think?"

He found himself unable to answer the question.

Because damn, her ass looked nice in those shorts. They weren't particularly short, but they hugged her curves.

"I should be going," he said abruptly. "Lots to do tonight."

"Of course. Don't let me keep you."

"Thank you for the cookies, by the way."

There was a strange feeling in his chest. He didn't know how to describe it.

Buoyancy, maybe?

Nah, that was ridiculous. She was just a pretty woman who lived next door and insisted on disrupting his quiet existence... and checking him out.

Nothing more than that.

But she'd made him smile. Very, very briefly.

[6]

On Saturday, it poured.

Not that it mattered to Victor. He didn't have any plans to leave the house. Nope, he'd just do a little work, exercise in his home gym, and watch Netflix.

He stared out the front window as he sipped his morning coffee.

It really was coming down out there. Why would anyone go out in this weather if they didn't need to?

A bright red umbrella popped into his view. It had black spots and little eyes protruding from the top.

A fucking *ladybug* umbrella. How completely unnecessary.

Even though he couldn't see her face, he knew exactly who was carrying that umbrella.

And then she tilted her umbrella and turned toward him. She had polka dot rainboots—of course she did. She smiled and waved, and he replied with a curt nod.

A moment later, his phone rang, and he picked it up.

"Ah, Victor! You finally answered," his mother said.

"I always answer when you call."

"No, that one time, you were in a meeting."

"That was three months ago." Victor ran a hand over his face and settled on an armchair.

"Do you live near Bloor?" Mom's voice boomed over the phone. She had a tendency to speak too loudly.

"Yes?"

"Wah, there was a shooting on Bloor. I heard it on the news. You must be careful. Toronto is such a dangerous city, I don't like you being there."

"Bloor is a long street," Victor said patiently. "I don't live anywhere near where that happened. Besides, Toronto is quite safe, but it has millions of people, so bad stuff is bound to happen on occasion."

"How far do you live from Bloor?" Mom demanded.

Victor sighed. "About a three-minute walk."

"Aiyah, too close. You should move."

"I'm not moving, Mom. We've been through this before."

"Sophia is talking about visiting you soon. I'm worried someone will kidnap her. She is so pretty, you know."

He hadn't had enough coffee for this.

"Sophia is welcome to visit." He'd like to see her, although he couldn't help hoping it would be a short visit so his youngest sister would have less time to meddle in his life. "She won't get kidnapped, I promise you. Kidnappings are extremely rare here."

But reasonable arguments wouldn't help. Mom would worry regardless. Her paranoia had increased in the past five years, ever since a totally improbable tragedy had befallen their family.

Victor worried more now, too, though not to the same extent. He didn't worry about Sophia getting kidnapped, but the other day, he'd pictured Amy perched on a pink bicycle with a basket full of flowers and a little puppy. He didn't know why that image had come to him, but it had immediately made a thread of fear snake through him.

No, Amy would be fine. Rainbows and unicorns and ladybug umbrellas would protect her wherever she went.

The sky flashed, quickly followed by a crack of thunder.

The lightning was close. And Amy was outside.

Goddammit, why was he worrying about her? He hardly knew her.

He returned his attention to the phone call. His mom was talking about candy.

"Do you eat pineapple candies?" She didn't wait for an answer. "They contain lead."

"All pineapple candies?"

"No, it is just one brand from China. I wrote down the name somewhere, but I can't find it now. You should stop eating all pineapple candies, just to be safe."

"Don't worry, Mom, I never eat pineapple candies."

"You are mocking me."

He sighed. He hadn't intended to use a mocking tone. He knew she was only trying to keep him safe.

"You don't have to worry so much." He'd said that so many times, even though there was no point.

"You cannot tell your mother not to worry. That is not how things work."

"I know."

"You will come home for Christmas this year, yes?"

"It's August. Christmas is more than four months away. I don't know yet. I might have lots of work to do."

"Aiyah! I know you are busy, but you must make time for us."

Yes, she'd lay on the guilt in every conversation now. Smart of her to start in August.

"Do you remember Lauren Kwong?" she asked.

He groaned and pinched the bridge of his nose. "Yes, I remember her."

"She is moving to Toronto. I told Brenda that she should not let her daughter move to Toronto, it is too dangerous there, but Lauren got a job. She is moving in September."

"Mm." It was obvious where this was going.

"I thought you could show her around the city. Look out for her."

"Mm-hmm."

"Victor!"

"Just say you want me to date her and marry her and make babies with her."

She gasped. "I would never interfere in your life that much." But then she laughed.

"Look, I can meet up with Lauren once, but I'm not dating her, okay?"

"Why not? She is a nice girl, and you are thirty-nine. It is past time. What are you waiting for? Wonder Woman?"

For some reason, Victor glanced out the window to where the ladybug umbrella had been earlier. "No."

"You took a long time to reply. Are you seeing someone at last?"

"No, I'm not seeing anyone, I swear. Do not get your hopes up, please."

"Too late," she said, "they are already up."

"You will just end up disappointed."

"Then don't disappoint me. Go out with Lauren. Or somebody. Anybody. I worry about you, all alone in that house. It is not good to be alone so much."

"I like it this way."

Plus, I have a cute neighbor who makes sure I don't get too much peace and quiet.

No way was he telling his mother about Amy.

Besides, it wasn't like there was anything to tell.

His mother clucked her tongue. "Okay, I will let you go now and give you more time to meet women."

"And eat poisoned candies. Right. Talk to you later."

~

Amy was still determined to make friends with her neighbor, but that was difficult since she hadn't seen him in a week, other than during that downpour when she'd foolishly felt like trying a matcha latte. He'd been standing at the window, and she thought she'd seen him nod at her.

She'd made it to Harbord Coffee Bar only partially wet—okay, mostly wet, though her rainboots had kept her feet dry. She'd talked to Lucy for a couple minutes, read for a while, and enjoyed her latte. It had almost been too pretty to drink, but eventually she'd managed.

Tonight was more pleasant. She was sipping tea on her patio after dinner, hoping that Victor would appear. She could, of course, knock on his door again, but she wasn't sure he'd appreciate that.

When she heard a sound from next door, she jumped up. Yes, there he was! Wearing a shirt, sadly, but—

Her phone vibrated. She had a video call.

"Hello, Abigail," Amy said as she stepped inside. She was a little disappointed that she wouldn't get to talk to Victor, but it was hard to be too disappointed. Her nieces were the best interruption she could think of.

"Auntie Amy, I got the card!" Abigail shoved the Ferris wheel pop-up card in front of her face. "It's addressed to *Miss* Abigail Sharpe." She seemed particularly pleased by that.

"Did your sisters get their cards, too?"

"Yes, but mine is the best. Do you want to hear a poem? I want to recite a poem for you."

"Sure. Let's hear it."

"Trick or treat, smell my feet, give me something good to eat. Not too big, not too small, just the size of Montreal."

"Abigail, you don't have to repeat that every five minutes."

Fred's voice. "Especially not in August. Wait, are you on the phone?"

"With Auntie Amy!"

"Give me the phone."

"Say 'please.'"

"Please give me the phone, Abigail."

"No, I want to say the poem again. In a *spooky* voice."

"Abigail…"

"Fine. Be that way. You won't get to hear me say it in my cool underwater voice."

"I think I'll live." Fred's face appeared on the screen. "How's Toronto?"

"Great!" Amy said.

"We had Janey babysit last Thursday."

"How did it go?"

Fred frowned. "Abigail was not happy. Apparently Janey didn't read *The Balloon Tree* properly like you do, whatever 'properly' means. Abigail was still up when we got home."

Don't feel guilty. Don't feel guilty.

"Anyway," he said, "I have to go. The twins just got out of the bath and I should help with that. Talk to you later."

Amy was relieved her brother didn't want to talk for long, but when she got back outside, Victor had already gone in.

Dammit.

But she had stuff to do. She'd noticed some unlabeled boxes in the basement when she and Sierra had moved a table down there the other day. She'd check what was in those, then likely throw them in the trash.

She opened the first box. It was full of fabric, some of which was likely decades old.

Amy had been meaning to start sewing. Aunt Frances had a sewing machine that looked to have been purchased within Amy's lifetime, and she figured she'd have a go at it. Might be fun.

None of these fabrics were anything she'd want to wear, but they could be good for practice, right? She'd keep that box.

The second box also contained fabric, so she expected the same in the third box.

She was surprised to find dozens of furry pink handcuffs instead.

Yes, Great Aunt Frances had kept a large box of handcuffs in her basement.

[7]

August sixteenth was not a good day.

At least it was a Friday this year. Victor could get drunk if he wanted, since nobody was expecting him at the office tomorrow. Although, to be honest, nobody would bat an eye if he occasionally didn't make it in until lunch.

He was on his third glass of scotch, and he was definitely tipsy. It was rare for him to have more than a single drink; he hadn't realized he'd become such a cheap drunk.

Or perhaps each of those three glasses had been more generous than intended.

Whatever.

His father had called earlier. Usually his mother made the phone calls, but this morning, it had been his father. They'd stumbled through the conversation for five minutes, not mentioning *it* at all.

The same thing had happened later this afternoon with Sophia. The last time she'd called rather than texted had been on his birthday, almost six months ago. They'd both known the reason for her phone call today, but they didn't say the words.

That was just the way it worked, and frankly, Victor was fine with it.

After dinner, he'd watered the cacti—although they probably hadn't needed it—and then he'd come out here with a bottle of scotch.

Unfortunately, twenty minutes ago, his neighbors had also come outside.

When he was sitting down, he couldn't see them over the fence, but he could recognize their voices.

There was Amy's laugh again. It was giving him a headache.

Why couldn't she go inside and leave him in peace?

Finally, the conversation next door faded away. Blessed silence. He had a gulp of his scotch, and it burned on the way down.

"Hey!"

He startled and spilled a bit of his drink.

"Sorry. I didn't mean to scare you." Amy was looking at him from the other side of the fence. "What are you doing?"

God, wasn't that obvious?

"Drinking," he muttered.

"What?"

"Scotch."

"Ooh, I've never had scotch before."

He hesitated. "Do you want to try some?"

She bounded inside her house, emerging several seconds later with…what the hell?

It was a ladybug mug.

"It matches your umbrella," he said.

"I love ladybugs."

"Of course you do."

"They have polka dots! What could be better?"

He didn't bother answering, even though hundreds of things came to mind. Instead, he picked up the bottle of scotch and walked over to her, stumbling against the fence.

"Are you okay?" she asked. "Too much to drink?"

"I'm fine."

"No need to drink alone. We can do it together."

"Thank you for the offer, but I'm perfectly fine. I'll just pour you a taste."

She laughed, and this time, the blasted noise didn't bother him.

Maybe he really was drunk, not just tipsy.

He leaned against the fence and took the mug from her hand. He was careful not to touch her fingers, afraid he would get infected with sunshine. She was wearing shorts again today, and if she turned around, he'd probably discover that her ass looked quite fine in them.

"Oh, that's more than enough!" she said.

Right. He was pouring her a drink.

He straightened the bottle and put on the lid.

"Cheers!" She held up her ladybug mug, and he helplessly clinked his glass against it. She tried a sip and made a face. "That's not what I expected."

Her expressions fascinated him. Her face was so open.

Amy wasn't artificially cheerful, and she didn't seem fake—or stupid. She was just naturally happy and excitable.

It was strange.

He wondered what that would be like, rather than being guarded all the time.

"Not a fan?" His voice became hoarse as he noticed the pink lipstick on her mug.

"Alcohol shouldn't taste like a bog."

"You prefer sweet, fruity cocktails?"

"Sometimes. Or wine. Or cider. I've recently discovered that cider can be exciting. My roommate took me to a place on Ossington, and I had a cider with strawberries and Earl Grey. It was delicious. Have you ever had strawberry Earl Grey cider?"

"I don't think such things belong in cider."

"Yet you're drinking this vile stuff that tastes like a peat bog."

He shrugged, suddenly questioning all of his life choices.

"What were you up to today?" she asked, resting her head in her hand.

She smiled at him as she waited for an answer, but he didn't want to answer that question. After half a minute, she gave up and started talking again.

"I had a great adventure," she said.

"Of course you did," he muttered.

"I took the subway over the Don Valley. It was neat when it went over the bridge. I didn't know there were any outdoor sections on the subway—I thought it was all underground."

"There are a few outdoor parts, yes."

"Did you grow up in Toronto?"

"No."

"Where are you from?"

"Edmonton." He tensed, worried that answer wouldn't satisfy her, worried she'd ask where he was *really* from.

He and his brother had been born in Hong Kong, but Victor barely remembered it. Edmonton was where he'd spent his childhood from the age of three onward.

There had been five kids. He and Christian were the oldest, then an eight-year gap between Christian and their first sister; Sophia was almost fifteen years younger than Victor.

Amy didn't question his answer. "It's cold in Edmonton, isn't it?"

"Yes. Colder than Toronto." He didn't miss that most of the time, although there was something about the bright blue sky and sunshine on a really, really cold day.

"Silver River is cold, too." She paused. "Anyway, my adventure today. I took the subway out east, then walked down to Gerrard and ate a dosa at an Indian restaurant. You ever had one?"

"No, I haven't."

"It's similar to a crepe," she said. "I got mine filled with some kind of potato, and it came with a bunch of chutneys. I don't know what they all were, but one had coconut and it was the best. Then I went to a coffee shop and had a latte with cardamom. It was really good. I love going to independent coffee shops in Toronto. They all have slightly different atmospheres, and I like to sip my drink and read a book."

"You managed to stop talking for more than ten minutes? How shocking."

Her eyes widened and her lips trembled.

Oh, hell. It was like kicking a puppy.

He felt terrible.

"Sorry," he said. "Ignore me. I'm having a bad day."

"Do you want to talk about it?"

My brother died five years ago today, and he was my best friend.

"No, I do not," Victor said instead.

"That's okay!" she said, upbeat now. "Do you want me to continue my story?"

He should say no. He'd just wanted to enjoy several glasses of scotch in solitude tonight, and she'd disrupted him.

Except he found himself nodding.

Amy was a lot to take, but he—grudgingly—enjoyed her excitement. And her pretty face.

"Excellent." She beamed. "I knew we were going to be friends."

Wait a second. This was all moving too fast.

When she reached across the fence and placed her hand on his upper arm, he froze.

Her hand was warm and soft, and he wanted to melt into her. Except there was a fence, and lots of other things, in the way.

"Sorry." She withdrew. "I invaded your personal space. I'm touchy-feely, and sometimes I forget that not everyone is the same. I'm trying to get better at it."

"It's okay," he said gruffly. "Just ask me next time."

"Do you want to come over? We can sit in my backyard and drink rather than standing by the fence."

"Uh, no." He didn't think that would be a good idea.

"Okay. I'll tell you my story here." She rested her arm along the top of the fence. "I came across a small Chinatown on Gerrard—I had no idea it was there. The archway with stone lions was kinda cool. Then I went back up Broadview to the Danforth, and I bought some Greek donuts with honey syrup."

He imagined honey coating her lips, dripping down her chin. He could lick it off.

"Oh, I almost forgot. Guess what else I found today?"

"I don't know. A llama with a flower crown on its head?"

Her laughter tinkled through the night.

God, he liked her laugh now. How strong was that scotch?

"You're hilarious." She reached out to touch him, then promptly pulled back her hand, respecting his boundaries. He appreciated it, but he felt a keen disappointment.

What was she doing to him?

"De Grassi!" she exclaimed.

It took him a moment to remember what she was talking about.

"I found De Grassi Street today," she said. "I hadn't realized it was a real place, and I came upon it by accident. Did you ever watch the shows?"

He shook his head.

"Of course not. It doesn't seem like your thing."

"My thing? You hardly know me."

"True. But I bet you watch scary crime shows." She shuddered.

If he watched a dark crime show with Amy, perhaps she'd cuddle up to him during the frightening bits...

She was really getting into his brain. He didn't understand it.

"I will neither confirm nor deny this," he said, his body leaning close to her out of its own accord. She smelled like honey and vanilla, and she was still holding that ridiculous ladybug mug...and he wanted to knock down the fence and pull her against him.

She took out her phone and showed him the De Grassi Street

sign. In the next picture, she was posing with it. She definitely looked cute in the photo, a wide smile on her face. Just like now.

"Anyway." She stuck the phone in her pocket. "That was my exciting day."

He grunted. "I'll live vicariously through you."

She laughed again. "Ooh, speaking of excitement, you'll never guess what I found in the basement!" She immediately clapped a hand over her mouth, and her cheeks turned pink. "Shit, I shouldn't have mentioned it."

Now he was intrigued. "What did you find?"

"Nope, my lips are sealed."

"Come on." For some reason, it was extremely important that she tell him.

"Not happening."

"I thought we were friends."

"Yes, I'm so glad you agree that we're friends! But I'm keeping my basement discovery a secret for now. I'll let you get back to drinking your peat bog alcohol in peace." She stepped away from the fence and waved at him as she approached her back door. "See you later."

Victor stared after her for several minutes.

What on earth had just happened? Why was he looking forward to the next time Amy disrupted his peace?

Dear God, this was disturbing.

Amy had last seen Great Aunt Frances several years ago, a few months before her grandmother's death.

It was the second time she'd driven Grandma to Toronto to visit her sister. It had been a bit of a struggle getting Grandma up the stairs to the house, but now Amy remembered having help from a neighbor, who'd looked a bit like Victor, come to think of it. But it definitely hadn't been Victor, because that man had been smiley and friendly and everything Victor was not, unless he'd had a personality transplant in the past few years.

Anyway, she and Grandma had visited Aunt Frances for the weekend, and it was fun to see Grandma with her sister, to hear them reminisce about their childhood.

There had been a tearful goodbye. Grandma's health was failing, and they weren't sure they'd get to see each other again.

And they hadn't.

Actually, the last time Amy had seen Aunt Frances was at her grandmother's funeral, but she barely remembered the funeral, had done her best not to think about it.

She really hadn't known the woman who'd left her the house very well, but that Sunday, she learned a little more.

She was heading out for a walk when she encountered Paula and Beast. When Beast saw Amy, her tail started wagging. She ran around Amy's legs and got herself tangled in her leash.

Amy bent down to untangle her. "Why hello, Beast. Who's a good girl?"

"*Woof, woof,*" Beast said.

"Where are you off to?" Paula asked.

Amy stood up. "I thought I'd head down to the lake."

"That's a long walk, but it's a lovely day. If you're going in that direction, you could also check out Frances's store."

Huh. "Aunt Frances had a store?"

"She transferred ownership to the manager when she got sick. You didn't know?"

Amy shook her head.

"Well, uh…" Paula seemed reluctant to share details, though she was the one who'd brought it up.

But how shocking could it be? Had Aunt Frances sold fine china? Teapot cozies?

And then Amy remembered the basement…

"It's called Pleasure," Paula said, "and it was one of Toronto's first sex shops."

[8]

THERE WAS a nice breeze off the lake, and lots of people were down here. Many were clearly tourists, but Amy wasn't a tourist.

No, she was a *local*.

But she hadn't been here long, and she kind of felt like a tourist.

Would she always feel that way in Toronto? It was just so big. There would always be new parts to explore.

She looked across the lake to the Toronto Islands. You could take a ferry out there, and one of them even had an amusement park.

Someday, she'd go.

For now, she headed to the Toronto Music Garden, one of the places she wanted to visit today. Perhaps there were more flowers earlier in the year, but it was still nice. She saw black-eyed Susans and echinacea. A willow tree. An area that looked like it was set up for concerts. There were signs with different musical terms, and a path that curled in a spiral. A couple was taking photos with a professional photographer—engagement photos, perhaps? The happy man and woman looked like they were about her age. The woman threw her head back and laughed, and somewhere in the distance, a child shrieked.

Amy lay down on a bench under some trees and used her hat as a pillow. It was a new hat that she'd bought at the mall yesterday, and it had a little bow on the side. She loved it, though the sheer quantity of people in the Eaton Centre had been overwhelming—she wasn't used to such crowds.

She didn't know how long she spent lying there in the warmth, but this was her month off. She could do whatever she wanted. Time wasn't important. Sure, she should probably start brushing up on her Fortran, but...

Amy awoke with a start. Huh. She must have dozed off.

Well, perhaps it was time to move on.

She passed boats docked at the marina, and a little while later, she arrived at Trillium Park, which was as far west as she'd intended to go. She sat on a rock by the water and looked out at the CN Tower and the rest of the skyline. What a lovely view! She took several pictures and uploaded one to Instagram.

By the time she started walking up Bathurst, she was hungry—and conveniently close to the banh mi place she'd been meaning to try. Her banh mi came with pork belly, shredded carrots, cilantro, and some kind of pickled vegetable. She pulled off the cilantro. Amy would eat almost anything, but cilantro had an unfortunate soapy taste.

She bit into her sandwich. God, it was good.

When she left the banh mi shop, a group of people walked by with black ice cream cones. One even had soft-serve black ice cream in their black cone.

Goth ice cream! How cool was that?

A minute later, she saw another couple with these distinctive black ice cream cones.

Amy hadn't planned to have ice cream today, but she had to check this out. She headed in the direction where the black ice cream cones were coming from and soon encountered a line-up.

She checked the sign. Sure enough, it was an ice cream shop, and apparently the color was from activated charcoal. She had no idea what that was, but she was going to try it anyway, even if it was a touch expensive and she had to wait in line behind a couple having an annoying argument about who should clean the bathroom.

Finally, she got to the front of the line. There were five flavors of soft serve. One was green tea and one was taro—she'd had those the other day, so she'd try something new. There were also genmaicha and mango, but she settled on the black ice cream, which was coconut flavored, with activated charcoal for good measure.

And she couldn't help getting rainbow sprinkles on her Goth ice cream, just because.

She took pictures of her ice cream in front of the white wall in the shop, and also in front of the pink wall of artificial flowers, which seemed to be made specifically for this purpose.

Then she went outside and licked her ice cream cone as she headed to her next destination. It was weird to be eating black ice cream. Her brain struggled with the fact that this was food. But wasn't it neat? The ice cream had a creamy coconut flavor—the activated charcoal didn't have much taste—and it wasn't quite as good as the taro ice cream at Ginger Scoops, but it was good nonetheless.

She was just crunching the last of her black cone when she arrived at Pleasure. She was curious to see the business that Great Aunt Frances had owned. And, okay, maybe there was another purpose for this stop, too.

Amy had never owned a vibrator, and she'd started wondering if this was a mistake.

She could get herself off without a vibrator. She didn't *need* one.

But it could be fun.

Of course, there had been no stores in Silver River that sold vibrators, though it would have been easy to order one online.

She walked inside. This was what sophisticated city women did, wasn't it? They had vibrators. They made their own pleasure.

Amy quickly located vibrators, dildos, flavored lube, body paint…and other things that she didn't understand.

Then she saw fuzzy handcuffs, identical to the ones in her basement.

Yep, this was definitely her great aunt's store.

After fifteen minutes, Amy had to admit she was lost. She had no idea what to look for in a vibrator, no idea what she would like. So, she mustered her courage and approached the middle-aged saleslady whose nametag said "Martha."

Normally, Amy wasn't nervous about approaching a stranger, but this was different.

"What can I help you with today?" Martha asked.

"I'd like to get a vibrator," Amy said. "What's a good, um, starter vibrator?"

Martha, of course, was very professional and not at all awkward. She spent a few minutes explaining the ins and outs of different options. The one she most highly recommended was rather expensive, but Amy decided to go for it.

Spending money in Aunt Frances's store and supporting the business was a noble cause, after all. The woman had left her a house in downtown Toronto. It was the least she could do.

Martha was ringing up the vibrator when she suddenly paused, tilted her head, and smiled. "I figured out how I know you."

Oh, dear. This was unexpected. "I'm new in town. I don't know anyone."

Martha opened the door behind her, and a minute later, she emerged with a photo frame.

Amy had never seen the picture before, but she recognized

the people in it: Grandma, Great Aunt Frances…and Amy. On the porch of what was now her house.

She vaguely recalled this photo being taken with Aunt Frances's old camera—not a digital camera, but one that required film—the last time she'd driven her grandmother to Toronto. The neighbor who looked like Victor had taken it at Aunt Frances's request.

"You're Frances's grandniece," Martha said. "She talked about you."

"Did she?"

"She appreciated all you did for her sister. Her sister used to brag about how you were so kind and smart. You're an engineer, aren't you?"

Amy nodded, feeling a bit embarrassed by the compliments.

"Sorry to make you uncomfortable," Martha said, "but I just had to say something. I want you to know the store is in good hands."

"I didn't even know she had a store until this morning."

"And now, here you are. I'll give you the employee discount."

"That's really not necessary."

"I insist."

Amy walked out a few minutes later with a bright pink vibrator, concealed in a plain white bag, and continued her walk.

Today had certainly been interesting.

As soon as Amy got home, she washed her new toy and lay down on her bed. She was curious—she had to try this right away.

She lifted up her skirt, slid off her underwear, and closed her eyes.

The image that immediately popped into her mind?

Victor cutting the grass.

No, she'd think of someone other than her neighbor...like Rebel. A fictional character. Yes, that was better.

She imagined his hard muscles rippling under his tattoos. An intense look on his face. The two of them could be on the run from demons, hiding in a closet, perhaps. He'd push up her skirt, just like this, and slide a finger inside her...

She turned on the vibrator at the lowest setting. It was extremely quiet, as the package promised—not that her house-mate was here now, anyway.

She pressed it to her clit and increased the speed, and with her other hand, she freed her breast from her clothes and circled her nipple, instinctively arching her back.

Oh, yes, that was good.

She imagined tracing his tattoos with her finger. Maybe rolling one of those honey-covered donuts over his tanned skin before popping it in his mouth. Then she'd lick the trail of honey, and he'd tip his head back, overcome by her touch, his eyes squeezed shut. Or maybe his gaze would be riveted on her because he found her so damn sexy.

Would he be good with his tongue?

Yes, she decided Victor—no, Rebel—was *very* good with his tongue. After she'd finished licking the honey off his chest, he'd give her a wicked smile and slide down her body. Then he'd leisurely lick her entrance as she gripped his hair and pressed him against her. He'd circle his tongue over her clit...

"Ohhh!" Amy cried out, her orgasm catching her off-guard.

Oh my.

She hadn't had an orgasm like that in a long time. This vibrator was certainly an amazing purchase, although perhaps the amazingness of the orgasm hadn't been entirely due to the toy.

Perhaps it was also because of the skill of Fantasy Victor.

No. *Rebel.* She'd been thinking about Rebel.

~

When Amy headed outside to read later that afternoon, she was in a particularly good mood. Even better, when she peeked over the fence, she saw Victor weeding his garden. His black T-shirt looked nice stretched over his back.

"Hey!" she said, expecting a brief nod in return.

But instead, he walked over to join her at the fence. "Hi."

That was when she realized her mistake.

She'd had a very hot masturbation session while thinking about a fictional character who just so happened to look a lot like her neighbor. And now he was standing a foot away from her, and she couldn't look him in the eye.

She kept thinking about the way he'd had his head between her legs…

Well, no matter. She'd plow forward.

"Guess what I did today?" she asked, not waiting for a response. "I walked down to the lake. Went to the Music Garden and Trillium Park. See?" She took out her phone and showed him a picture of the skyline from Trillium Park. "Then I had banh mi for the first time, which was delicious. I also had Goth ice cream." She flipped to a picture of her black ice cream.

"You got rainbow sprinkles on it," he murmured. "Of course you did."

His eyes met hers, and they flared with heat…or was it her imagination?

Regardless, she clenched her thighs together.

God, he really did look good up close.

"And then I…" Well, she wasn't going to tell him about the next thing she'd done. "There's a little market at Bathurst and Dundas. Tiny businesses in shipping containers—isn't that cool? Not all of them were open today, but I got something called turon at the Filipino one. Little spring rolls filled with banana, and they were soooo good."

"Yes, I do like those."

He was still looking at her intently, and she felt strangely aware of every inch of her body and every inch of his.

And that fence between them.

And the fact that he hadn't liked it when she'd touched him.

"There's just so much to eat in Toronto, and I'm going to try it all!" she said. "I found a restaurant that serves two dozen varieties of poutine. Isn't that interesting? I'm going to try at least three. There's a fancy hotdog place not far from here, plus an Italian restaurant with a great patio that's supposed to be excellent. God, I love pasta. Do you like pasta? There's also a tapas place near the cider bar that looked kind of cool. Plus a Cuban restaurant…"

Oh, dear. Victor looked like he was struggling to keep up with her verbal diarrhea. In fact, he seemed oddly fixated on her mouth.

She should probably stop talking.

"I'll let you get back to your reading!" she said cheerily. "Weeding, I mean. You were weeding. I'm going to read." She held up her e-reader. "I'm about to start a new book." She turned and waved at him over her shoulder.

Man, she must have made an utter fool of herself.

When she looked back at the fence, Victor was gone.

"Oh, no," Amy murmured. "No, no, no."

She'd been sending her father a text—reminding him that his wedding anniversary was tomorrow—when the smoke detector went off. She hurried to the hallway, climbed on a stool, and pulled the battery out of the smoke detector. Then she ran to the kitchen. It was, indeed, a little smoky.

She pulled out the chicken casserole, which looked okay. As it should. She'd made this many times before—it was her grandma's recipe—and knew exactly how long it took.

The Brussels sprouts, on the other hand, were charred.

Usually Amy and Sierra ate separately, but she'd thought having Sunday dinners together would be nice. Amy had volunteered to cook the first one, and she'd decided to make Brussels sprouts to surprise her roommate. She'd looked at recipes until her head was spinning, then decided not to follow them. She'd thrown the Brussels sprouts into the oven with maple syrup and a few other things, planning to add bacon and cheese at the end.

So much for that.

Ugh. Amy really wanted to do something nice for her housemate. She tried a Brussels sprout, just in case it was okay. It was burnt all the way through—she couldn't serve this to Sierra. She'd have to toss them.

"What happened?" Sierra asked, coming into the kitchen with the vacuum cleaner.

"I burnt the Brussels sprouts I was making for you. I'm sorry. Don't worry, there's still lots of food. Chicken casserole and berry crumble."

"You made all that for me?"

"And me."

"I'm sure the rest of it will be great. I'll put the vacuum away then be right back."

They sat down to dinner five minutes later. It was nice to have someone else around, to eat dinner together and hang out. They each had their own chores to do—they'd divvied up the household ones—and there had been no problems so far.

Sierra dug into the chicken casserole with gusto. The smell of burnt vegetables permeated the air, but otherwise, it was a pleasant dinner.

"You still liking Toronto?" Sierra asked.

"Yes, it's great. Lots of food. Interesting buildings and other things to see. Hoping to visit the Flatiron Building and the dog fountain in Berczy Park this week. Though occasionally I get overwhelmed by all the people, like when I went to the Eaton Centre."

"Yeah, it can be a zoo. All the people enjoying the air conditioning in the hot weather."

"I can't imagine what Christmas would be like." Amy paused for a bite of food. "I'm still having trouble sleeping. Not all the time, but I can't fully adjust to the noise."

"I lived on a major street before, so I'm actually enjoying the peace here. I'll give you my fan. It's the world's noisiest fan and generates very little air flow, but it's great as a white-noise generator."

"Thank you. That would be awesome. I should have thought of something like that."

"I'll get it after dinner. Then, do you want to watch a movie? *While You Were Sleeping?*"

"I've never seen that one."

"No?" Sierra said. "Okay, we're definitely watching it. Maybe I'm in the mood for it because I'm thinking about dating again. I'm setting up a profile on one of those dating apps."

"Ooh, let me know if you need help with your profile."

"I might have to take you up on that."

"I'll be sure to add that you love Brussels sprouts and make lovely cards." Amy grinned.

"By the way, how's it going with Victor? I know you said you're just being friendly—"

"I think I'm succeeding. We actually have conversations now. Sure, I do the majority of the talking, but still. I..."

Amy trailed off as her cheeks heated and she remembered what she'd done earlier that afternoon. And the awkward conversation with Victor afterward.

Sierra raised her eyebrows, looking amused, but she didn't say anything.

"Ready for berry crumble?" Amy asked.

[9]

VICTOR HAD SPENT a lot of time in his backyard lately.

It was mid-August, and the weather was nice. He liked sitting outside with a cup of coffee or a glass of scotch and staring at the garden. It helped to clear his mind.

It had nothing to do with hoping he'd see Amy. No, absolutely nothing.

"Hey!" Her head popped up above the fence.

He refused to smile as he walked toward her, cup of coffee in hand.

"How was your day?" he asked.

"Not too exciting. Met with my supervisor, did a little cleaning."

"No black ice cream with sprinkles?" It rather amused him that she talked about food all the time.

"For once, I didn't buy any food or drink when I was out, though I nearly got an apron. I already have an apron, but this one was light blue with cherries and red trim. Kind of retro, you know? But after my big purchase on Sunday…" She trailed off and her cheeks pinkened slightly.

"What did you buy?"

She shook her head.

Strange that she didn't want to tell him, when she usually talked a *lot*. On Sunday, for example, she'd talked so fast that he'd barely been able to follow her.

Intriguing.

"Anyway," she said, "I should be going."

He wasn't disappointed. No, going to the office each day was enough social interaction for him.

Wasn't it?

Something curious happened on Wednesday.

Victor was outside, having his pre-dinner coffee, when he heard the back door slide open next door.

He waited a minute. Nobody spoke to him.

Huh.

His phone buzzed and he checked his message.

It was from his mother. A picture of the pineapple candies that he wasn't supposed to eat, not that he liked pineapple anyway. The only things he liked with "pineapple" in the name were pineapple buns, and those didn't have any actual pineapple in them.

They'd been his and Christian's favorite.

He walked over to the fence. "Amy?"

She startled and knocked something off the table.

Fortunately, it wasn't her laptop.

Because yes, she had her laptop out there with her, as well as several notebooks.

"Sorry," he said. "What are you up to?"

"I'm studying."

"Okay, I won't bother you then." He started to turn away.

"No, come on over and chat before I start working."

He hadn't gone to her backyard the last time she'd invited

him, and he hesitated, then decided to do it. Just five minutes. It would hardly count as socializing.

When he got to her backyard, she gestured to the chair beside her, so he sat down.

"I'm relearning Fortran," she said.

"Oh?"

"I need it for my project. It'll involve reviewing and modifying some old code that was written in Fortran, and I haven't programmed since school. We did Java in first year, and there was a class with some Fortran later on. I don't remember it at all, though I do remember that I struggled at first, but eventually I got the hang of it. I'm sure I'll be able to manage. Just going over my old notes and getting myself in the right mindset, you know?"

"I bet you'll be fine, but you can ask me if you need help," he said before he knew what he was doing. "That's what I do for a living. I'm a software developer."

"You are? That's cool. Do you use Fortran?"

"Not in a long time, but…"

He trailed off, and she didn't say anything. They were both looking down at their thighs, which were nearly touching.

It was strange to see her without a fence in the way. Her skin was so close to his. He wanted to reach out and pull her onto his lap—he was sure that would elicit a laugh. Then he'd set his mouth to hers, so she couldn't talk…

God, why was he thinking of kissing this woman who baked cookies and skipped in the rain with a ladybug umbrella and put rainbow sprinkles on black ice cream?

Christian would have laughed his ass off.

Amy was nothing like Victor, and sometimes she irritated the fuck out of him. There was a unicorn pencil case beside her laptop, with the words "Never stop dreaming."

Yet, he wanted to tumble onto the grass with her and sink inside her.

And her breasts were a thing of beauty in that low-cut T-shirt.

"Um." He ran a hand through his hair. "I should cook dinner. See you later."

"Bye, Victor!" she called as he hurried back to the safety of his own backyard.

～

The next day, Victor cut the grass.

Strictly speaking, he didn't need to cut the grass. He could wait until the weekend. But, whatever, it was sunny, and he felt like being outside. He took off his shirt, even though it wasn't as disgustingly hot as it had been the past few days.

When he turned off the lawn mower, he glanced next door, and he couldn't help the pleasure that swelled in him when he saw Amy staring at him, her lips parted.

Yeah, he'd been uncomfortable with the way his thoughts had been heading yesterday, but how could he not be pleased when a gorgeous woman was looking at him like that?

He stalked toward her, and she continued to look at him, her gaze never once faltering.

"Amy." He stopped when he was very close to the fence. "How are you doing?"

She swallowed. "I'm good. Yes, I'm good."

"Why, exactly, are you good?" He slid one finger under her chin and tipped her head up.

"I'm just a cheerful person! You must have noticed."

"Well, 'cheerful' isn't how I'd describe you right now."

Why was he pushing this? He couldn't seem to help it.

He adjusted his stance. His cock was getting hard. She was wearing the blue dress with white polka dots today, and... Oh, fuck. The dress had tiny buttons all the way down. Here he was in old black shorts with a drawstring, nothing else, and she was wearing a fucking dress with a dozen buttons.

Wouldn't those be fun to undo?

He bet she'd be very enthusiastic in the bedroom—or on the grass. She'd have sex as enthusiastically as she did everything else.

God, it had been a damn long time, but his hand would have to be enough tonight.

She made a soft gasp as he touched the tip of his finger to the edge of her lips. Just that simple touch was enough to make heat sizzle all the way through him.

Jesus, he really needed to get laid.

This was one of the unfortunate side effects of being a recluse: opportunities to get physical with a woman were rare.

And using an app?

Just shoot him now.

Though perhaps he should consider it.

Dammit, why did Amy still have her lips parted? It was driving him nuts. He wanted to poke his tongue between her lips and slide it over hers.

But then she closed her mouth, and that was no better. She looked just as tempting.

He removed his hand and noted the tiny bit of red lipstick on his fingertip.

Dear God.

"I was admiring you!" she said at last.

He hadn't expected that honesty, though he supposed it wasn't out of character.

"Is that so?" he said.

"Yes! You know you're all muscly, doing physical labor…I can't help it."

She was such a goddamn delight.

"Mm-hmm." He leaned closer.

Wait, was he about to kiss her? Kiss a woman who owned a pencil case that said "Never stop dreaming"?

He stepped back and gestured to his lawn. "I should, uh, trim the edges."

"Trim the edges! Yes, that's exactly what you should do." She waved at him and stepped away from the fence. "Have fun."

Well, any "fun" he had would be because he couldn't help thinking about those blasted buttons on her dress. He wondered what she would have done if he'd kissed her and undone the top button. He rather wished…

No, he did not.

It was embarrassing enough that he'd leaned forward.

In the next week, Victor spent quite a bit of time outside, and he had a five-minute conversation with Amy nearly every day, either in the late afternoon or evening.

It was not the highlight of his day.

No, he definitely wouldn't say that.

On Thursday, he checked the mail and discovered that a letter for Amy had been delivered to his address instead.

Miss Amy Sharpe. So that was her full name. Not Amy Glitter-bomb, or whatever the fuck he'd been imagining. It didn't look like a bill; no, the address was written in pen, and the return address was in Silver River. In fact, it looked like it had been written by a child.

He might as well deliver this right away, so he headed next door and rang the doorbell.

Amy answered a few seconds later.

"Hey!" She grinned. She looked happy to see him.

Which was kind of nice, he supposed.

"You got a letter," he grunted. "It was delivered to my address by mistake."

She reached out, and he handed it over. "It's from my niece." Then she tilted her head and gave him an odd look. "You rang my doorbell rather than putting it in the mailbox. That's a very friendly thing to do."

He scratched the back of his neck. It had never occurred to him to just put the letter in her mailbox. Why not? That would have been the sensible action.

"If you don't have any plans for the long weekend," she said, "how would you like to have lunch on Saturday?"

"*Lunch?*" he sputtered.

"I have a few ideas. There's a taco place in Kensington Market that I've been meaning to try. Also, a deli that does Montreal smoked meat sandwiches. Or dim sum—I've never had dim sum. Sierra told me about a great restaurant, but she can't go with me this weekend because she's working."

His head was spinning. "Are you asking me on a date?"

"No, this is a friendly lunch." She brushed some hair out of her eyes. Her hair was down today, and it looked a bit wet—had she just gotten out of the shower?

He crossed his arms over his chest. "The way you were looking at me when I cut the grass was hardly what I call *friendly*. You were checking me out. You called me *muscly*."

"I did. That's true." She put a finger to her chin, as though thinking. "But you can't talk."

"What?"

"I saw the way you were looking at me, too." She smiled at him, rather coquettishly. It was different from any smile he'd seen on her before.

And damn, it made blood rush to…certain parts.

"I…was not…" he stammered.

"But you were! And you touched my mouth."

"I did not touch your mouth."

"You did."

"I touched the corner of your lips. Not the same."

They stood there, facing each other. Something electric zinged between them, and he wanted to touch the corner of her lips again. Or push her up against the door.

But, no.

Victor had self-control. Self-control was one of his strengths.

Although his did seem to be slipping a bit lately.

"It's the same," she said quietly, but with firmness.

He didn't know how to extricate himself from this conversation.

Amy's usual smile returned. "Anyway, would you like to go out for a friendly meal this Saturday?"

"Sure. We can have dim sum."

He hadn't had dim sum in a long time. He typically ate alone, and dim sum was hard to eat alone because everything came in servings of three or more.

That was the only reason he'd agreed to have dim sum with Amy.

Of course it was.

[10]

"This is so exciting!" Amy said as she skipped along the sidewalk.

She was going to eat food she'd never had before, and, more importantly, she was going to do it with Victor.

Amy had been determined to become friends with him, and she'd succeeded.

She'd also succeeded in…

No, she would not think of what she'd done with her vibrator under the covers last night. That vibrator sure had gotten a lot of use lately. Why hadn't she bought one sooner?

"You're…skipping." Victor strolled beside her, hands shoved in his pockets. He was wearing jeans and a button-down short-sleeve shirt.

Amy was wearing her sunflower dress, which she couldn't help remembering was what she'd been wearing the first time they'd met.

And although she really was excited, she was skipping just because she thought it would annoy him, and for some reason, he looked extra hot when she got under his skin.

"Skip with me!" she said.

He gave her an utterly horrified look.

She started walking like a normal person. She'd had her fun.

"Alright, this is the place." She stopped in front of a restaurant in Chinatown.

They walked inside, and Victor said something to a server in a language that wasn't English. Cantonese? She hadn't known he spoke Cantonese.

The small restaurant was loud and crowded, and it was quite different from the Chinese restaurant she'd gone to occasionally in Sudbury. They were seated at a table near the back. A pot of tea was immediately brought over and placed on the plastic tablecloth.

"Ah, this is one of the places with carts," Victor said.

"I thought dim sum restaurants always had carts."

"Nah, in a lot of places, you order off the menu."

A little old lady shuffled by, pushing a cart full of steamers and saying something Amy didn't understand.

Victor stopped her and said a few words, and she placed two steamers in front of them. She scribbled something on a piece of paper on their table, which Amy hadn't noticed before.

"What is it?" she asked as he lifted the lids. Steam rose, and she breathed in the aroma.

"Har gow and char siu bao. Shrimp dumplings and barbecued pork buns. Sorry, I forgot to ask, is there anything you don't like or can't eat?"

"I'll eat pretty much anything. Except liver, olives, and cilantro."

He nodded and deftly picked up a dumpling with his chopsticks.

Amy, well, she failed at using chopsticks. She tried her best, but these were slippery suckers. She'd have to get better at this.

The shrimp dumpling was juicy and delicious, though. Next, she went for a piece of pork bun.

"Do you like it?" he asked.

"Yes! It's really good."

He gave her a slight smile, which was as much smiling as Victor ever did, and it was impossible not to notice his forearms when she was sitting across the table from him.

You're friends, she reminded herself. *He's your neighbor.*

Another dish was placed on their table.

"Cheong fun," Victor said as the server poured something on top—it looked like soy sauce. "Rice noodle rolls. These ones have beef."

Again, Amy failed with her chopsticks, so she used her spoon. She'd barely gotten the first piece in her mouth when Victor asked for something else. A set of three items that were somewhat spherical.

"Taro dumplings," he said.

"Ooh, it looks like spun sugar. I had taro ice cream the other day, and it was tasty."

"These are savory. There's pork inside."

Amy eagerly tried one. She didn't like it as much as the other items, but it was still pretty good.

Yet another plate appeared on their table.

"Okay, you might have to stop ordering things for a while," Amy said.

The table was full, and Victor was transferring the shrimp dumplings into the barbecued pork bun steamer.

"I just want you to try everything." He looked almost sheepish as he stacked the steamers on top of each other.

"What are these?" she asked, pointing at the new plate.

"Sesame balls."

She reached for one with her fingers. When she bit into it, the inside was partly hollow, but there was some kind of sweet paste.

"Lotus," Victor said.

She didn't know what that was, but she'd look it up later.

Sesame *balls*.

For some reason, that amused her. She was so juvenile.

And she was here with Victor, who was quietly eating across from her. She was obsessed with watching him put things in his mouth.

She bounced in her chair as she reached for another shrimp dumpling.

He gestured at her with his chopsticks. "It looks exhausting. Being excited all the time."

"I'm just enjoying my new life in Toronto." Perhaps she shouldn't be so easily entertained, though—he probably thought she was an unsophisticated small-town girl—but she couldn't seem to help it.

"What was your life like in Silver River?" He helped himself to a sesame ball.

"It wasn't too bad, but I didn't love it. There's not much to do in the town. I spent a lot of time with my family, often babysitting my three nieces."

"How many siblings do you have?"

"Two brothers. You?"

He hesitated. "I'm the oldest of five."

"Five! That's a lot. Anyway, they always wanted me to help with stuff, and I'm not very good at saying no."

"It's important to be able to say no."

"It is, but I'm so bad at it. I want everyone to like me. Something that doesn't seem to matter to *you*."

"And you saw me as an extra challenge, because I didn't immediately love you?"

She shrugged, not wanting to admit how he made her feel.

"I had a boyfriend, too," she said. "Shane and I broke up a few months before I inherited the house."

There was a flash of...something in Victor's eyes, and she couldn't help being pleased, even though it shouldn't matter to her at all.

"I doubt Shane would have wanted to move to Toronto," she continued, "and he wouldn't have helped organize the move or done much in the way of chores. I suspect if we'd lived together, I would have been nagging him to do the bare minimum. Our relationship was rather one-sided, but I didn't see it for the longest time. Didn't realize that I was the one planning every date, every Valentine's Day. All of my romantic relationships have been that way. My other relationships, too. Like my family. Nobody gives me much in return." She sighed. "Maybe it's petty of me to say that. They're family."

"No, it's fair. They take you for granted."

"Moving to Toronto felt very selfish of me."

"You need to do things for yourself sometimes."

"Exactly. I'm enjoying it so much."

"Glad to hear it." He didn't sound *glad*, but he'd said the words, and Victor wasn't the kind of guy who'd lie about things like that. She might lie to make people feel better, but he wouldn't.

"It's like a big vacation," she said, "except I get to live here. How awesome is that?"

He grunted in acknowledgement, but it wasn't an unhappy grunt. Then he stopped an elderly Chinese woman and asked for a steamer from her cart.

"Victor, we still have so much food," Amy said.

"But you can't have dim sum for the first time without siu mai."

"What's in it?"

"Pork, prawn, mushroom…not sure what else."

"What's the orange stuff on top?"

"Looks like roe. Sometimes it's carrot instead."

Ooh. That sounded interesting. This time, she managed to pick it up with her chopsticks.

Oh my God. It tasted amazing.

"This is my favorite so far," she said, then realized she hadn't finished chewing.

Crap. She was having her first *friendly* meal with Victor, and she was being rude.

She reached for more siu mai. "What are you up to for the rest of the weekend?"

He shrugged.

"Let me guess," she said. "You're going to sit outside and brood while you drink scotch that tastes like a bog."

He shrugged again.

Damn, this man could be irritating at times.

But she did like him. As a *friend*.

"Are you going to cut the grass shirtless?" she asked.

He raised his eyebrows. "You wish."

Why was he so sexy when he spoke like that? It was unfair how sexy he could be.

"What are you doing this weekend?" he asked.

Excellent. A nice question to distract her.

"I'm going out with my roommate tonight," she said, "and I've got to prepare to start grad school on Tuesday. I'm looking forward to it. I love school."

"Of course you do."

"You didn't like school?"

"My grades were fine, but I was glad to be done."

"Well, I always meant to go back, and I'm glad to have the chance."

"Are you going to get a PhD eventually?" he asked.

"It's not the plan, but it's an outside possibility, yes."

"You'd make a hot professor."

Her face prickled. "There aren't many tenure-track positions. Way fewer than the number of people with PhDs."

"I'm aware."

"And you just called me *hot*."

He shrugged once more. "You know I'm attracted to you. No sense hiding it now."

It suddenly seemed really, really warm in here. There was no air conditioning, was there?

Victor kept eating as though he hadn't said anything of note, and she continued to stare at him as he refilled her tiny teacup, then got them another plate of food. Fried squares of…she wasn't sure what.

"Turnip cake," he said.

She frowned. "Remember when you asked what I didn't like? I forgot to mention turnip."

"I think it's actually some kind of radish."

She tried it. It wasn't her favorite, but she was glad she'd gotten a taste. She'd let Victor eat the rest of it.

She pointed at some tarts on a passing cart. "What are those?"

"Egg tarts."

"Let's get them, and then I think we'll have enough."

When it was time to pay, Victor grabbed the bill and handed over some cash before she realized what was happening.

"I invited you out," she said. "I was going to pay."

"Tough luck."

She gave him a look, and for some reason, it made him laugh. He rarely laughed, and this was a bigger laugh than she'd ever heard from him before. His eyes crinkled, and he looked so…

Well, he looked sexy no matter what he did.

They headed outside into the heat, and she half-wanted to ask him to extend this non-date with coffee and roll cake, but she was too full. As they walked home, she made inane comments here and there because she couldn't help herself.

But she was always very *aware* of him.

When they stopped on the sidewalk in front of their houses and he said, "So I guess this is it?" she wanted to pull him against her and kiss him.

Instead, she said, "Thank you for having dim sum with me."

"Thank you for inviting me," he said, somewhat gruffly.

Then there was silence. Amy was usually the one to fill silence, yet no words came out.

She looked down at those fabulous forearms.

But he was her neighbor and she'd only intended to be friends with him. Besides, she'd just told him about Shane, her last boyfriend, and that relationship hadn't worked out well at all.

Still, she leaned forward, and she thought he leaned forward too, just the tiniest bit.

And then her brain realized what she was doing, and she skipped over to her porch.

"See you later!" She waved.

Amy couldn't stop thinking about Victor all day.

She thought about him when she was in her room, reviewing old Fortran assignments.

She thought about him while reading in the cozy reading nook on the second floor.

She thought about him while reading outside on the patio with a mug of tea.

She thought about him as she sorted through the fabric from the two boxes in the basement and set up the sewing machine on the third floor.

And she thought about him while she was out for beers with Sierra.

She'd met Sierra at eight o'clock at a craft beer bar in Kensington Market called A Pint or Two. Amy had never drunk at a "craft beer bar" before. Shane would have rolled his eyes at a bar that refused to serve Labatt or Molson, but Amy was enjoying her saison. Earlier, she'd had a stout brewed with donuts. She wouldn't have guessed there were donuts if she hadn't known, but it was good.

Sierra drained her IPA. "One last beer? It's such a nice night out."

It was indeed a lovely night. They were sitting on the patio, the noises of the city surrounding them. Amy was coming to love the background noise of Toronto. Not the sirens, but the traffic, the rattle of the streetcar on Spadina. All the conversations around them. And thanks to Sierra's loud fan, the sounds of the city weren't affecting her sleep much anymore.

Normally, Amy would say yes, another beer would be great. There was a raspberry sour that she was curious to try.

However, she couldn't stop thinking of Victor.

Would he be sitting alone in his backyard, a glass of scotch in hand?

"No, let's head out," she said. "You have to work tomorrow."

Sierra raised an eyebrow. "I don't open the store until noon on Sundays, and we'll still be home by midnight."

"Um, well…"

"You want to see him, don't you?"

"Who are you talking about?"

"You know exactly who I mean. Our neighbor. The one you had dim sum with today."

"Yeah, sure, I guess." Amy laughed. She couldn't manage to sound blasé.

"Alright, we'll head out once you're done your beer."

When they got home, Sierra winked at Amy, and Amy immediately went out back, her heart beating faster than usual. She peeped over the fence…and there he was. He was mostly in the shadows, but his face was partially illuminated by the lights at the back of the house. Sure enough, he had a glass of scotch in hand.

"Hey," she said. "You look like you could use some company."

He turned to her, and she couldn't speak. God, he was so gorgeous. She'd thought he was hot when she first met him, but that feeling had only intensified in the past few weeks.

"I've already socialized today. I had a meal with someone earlier." His eyes seemed to bore into hers.

"Oh, well, if you don't—"

"Come on over, Amy."

By the time she'd gotten to his backyard, he'd set out a chair for her. She'd never been in his yard before. It was rather exciting.

She couldn't help herself from moving her chair as close to his as possible.

"So, what have you been up to in the past"—he looked at his watch—"ten hours?"

"Got a bunch of chores done, then had a couple beers with my housemate."

And thought about you a lot.

But she didn't say that, of course.

Except from the way he was looking at her now, it felt like he knew her secret.

He raised his glass to his lips and had a swallow, then put the glass down on the table beside him. "You want a drink?"

She shook her head and watched his Adam's apple bob as he swallowed again.

"You said I'd make a hot professor earlier."

He chuckled softly. "So I did."

He was staring out at the garden, not at her, and he said nothing more.

She wanted him to look at her. She wanted a hell of a lot more than that, if she was honest with herself. The thought sent warning bells ringing in her head, but she couldn't seem to help wanting him.

"Victor." She placed her hand on the arm of his chair.

His gaze snapped toward hers, and it was suddenly hard to breathe. He inched his hand toward hers but didn't touch it.

"May I sit on your lap?" she asked.

He spun his glass in his other hand. "Would you like to sit on my lap in a *friendly* way? Like how we had a *friendly* meal together earlier?"

"No, not like that."

The next few seconds seemed to last an eternity.

Then he tilted his head. "Come here."

She settled on his lap, her knees bent on either side of his hips. Her sunflower dress hiked up a little as she straddled him.

He inhaled swiftly.

She'd known he was attracted to her, but hearing that... Well, it definitely made her feel good about herself.

"Is this chair going to collapse from our combined weight?" she asked.

"It'll be fine," he said hoarsely. "How can you think about the structural integrity of the chair right now?"

Both of his hands were in her hair, gently brushing it as he looked into her eyes like it was impossible to look anywhere else.

There were goose bumps on her skin, despite the warm air.

"You're beautiful," he said quietly.

And then he kissed her.

His lips brushed over hers, so softly, the pressure increasing as she kissed him back and melted into him. He tasted slightly of scotch but she enjoyed the peat bog taste like this. Enjoyed everything right now. All the places where her body pressed against his —it felt amazing.

She was about to slip her tongue into his mouth, but then he pulled back.

"Okay?" he asked as he rubbed circles at the base of her jaw with his thumbs.

"More than okay." She wiggled her hips and... Oh, God. She could feel his erection.

He growled before kissing her again, with more urgency than the first time. His hands shifted down to grab her ass and press her tightly against him, and she responded by wrapping her arms around his shoulders and kissing him back just as hard.

He touched his tongue to hers, and she moaned. She'd had fantasies about having his tongue all over her, and the real thing was even better. She slipped her hands under his shirt and scraped her fingernails over his skin, and then it was his turn to moan, a moan which seemed to reverberate inside her.

It felt so good…and physical.

Yet it was more than that.

She cupped his jaw in her hand. Their kiss became more desperate, like they were trying to get ever closer and it just wasn't close enough.

Could he tell how wet she was? Only the thin fabric of her panties was against his jeans.

She tore her mouth away and looked at him. They were both panting.

And with the tiniest bit of distance, her mind started to function again.

She could take him inside her, and she was sure she'd enjoy it. But they'd only kissed for the first time five minutes ago—had it been five minutes? She had no concept of time. And that kiss been enough to turn her world upside down.

"Amy," he murmured, nuzzling her neck. "What do you want?"

"Just this," she whispered. "Nothing more than this."

"I can do that." He placed a delicate kiss to her earlobe, then a slightly less delicate one to her chin, making his way to her lips.

Okay. This was good. Safe.

They kissed each other in his backyard for a long time. Just kissing, though it was hardly "just" anything.

When she finally went inside, she was surprised to see it was after midnight, and all the lights were off—Sierra had gone to sleep.

Amy felt different than she had last night as she brushed her teeth, washed her face, and put on her pajamas.

She'd kissed Victor.

Before she turned out the light, she took her new vibrator out of her night table.

[11]

"Do you buy chicken burgers?" Mom asked.

Victor pulled the phone away from his ear—his mother was talking too loudly again—and nodded as the bartender placed a beer in front of him.

"No, I don't eat chicken burgers," Victor said.

"If you do, you must be careful."

"Mom, I—"

"There was a man in Calgary, he thought the frozen chicken burgers that come in a box are already cooked. Because of the breading, I guess? He just microwaved them for a minute to heat them up. Then he got sick and ended up in the hospital."

"Don't worry." Victor had a sip of his beer. "I always cook my chicken thoroughly."

"I had to warn you about the burgers, in case you didn't know they were raw."

"But I told you, I don't eat chicken burgers anyway."

"Well, you might start," she said. "And I did not teach you what to do in the kitchen, so I must make up for it now. You should be careful with romaine lettuce, too. Sometimes it has e-coli."

"Yes, there was a recall last year, I remember."

"You know, I was reading an article about how some young women do not want to get married because they do not want to look after a man. Apparently, many men expect their wives to be like their mothers."

"Why are you bringing this up?"

"Because maybe this is why women are not interested in you. They think you need too much mothering."

"I do not. I'm perfectly capable of looking after myself." He thought of Amy and what she'd said about her ex.

"Have you called Lauren Kwong?"

He glanced around the bar to see if Jay was here yet. Still no sign of his friend.

"No," Victor said. "Look, I'm out right now. Can we talk later?"

"You should call her."

"She's been in Toronto, what, all of two days? I'll give her some time to get settled." He intended to get in touch with Lauren eventually because he would never hear the end of it otherwise. But he also intended to make it clear that he had no interest in her like *that*.

Now that he'd said he had to go, his mom would probably see it as her cue that there were five to ten minutes left in the conversation.

"Sophia booked her ticket to Toronto," Mom told him. "Did you know?"

"Yes, she forwarded me the information."

"She said she got a good deal on the flight and—"

Jay Sampson sat down across from Victor.

Victor gave him a brief nod. "Mom, I really do have to go. My friend is here."

"You are saying 'friend,' but do you actually mean a date?"

"No, my friend is here."

"You are speaking weirdly."

"No, I'm not. I'll talk to you soon." He ended the call and slid his phone into his pocket.

"How's your mother?" Jay asked with a chuckle. "Same as usual?"

"Yeah."

Jay had met Christian in university. Many of Victor's friends had been Christian's friends first.

Okay, saying Victor had "many" friends was a stretch. He went out to a bar to socialize maybe a few times a year. Last time Jay had texted him, Victor had said no, but two days ago…well, he'd figured it might be nice.

Jay had a wife and two young children, so they talked about Jay's family for a bit, and then Jay leaned forward, hand around his pint, and said, "So, what's up with you, man? You look good. Relaxed."

Victor stared at his friend, appalled by the idea that he looked "good and relaxed."

He felt like Jay could see exactly what he'd been up to the past three nights with Amy.

Because, yes, it had happened more than once.

Every night, by silent agreement, they both went outside when it was dark. Sometimes he saw her earlier in the backyard, but she only came over for a "friendly" sit on his lap once night had fallen.

His lips twitched.

"Is that a smile I see?" Jay asked.

"No, definitely not," Victor said.

"Pretty sure it was."

"Amused at my mom's lecture on food safety and chicken burgers, that's all."

"Mm-hmm. You met someone, didn't you?"

"Nah, I don't know what you're talking about."

Unfortunately, Jay must have perfected his "tell me the truth" dad look in the past several months, and Victor found himself cracking against his will.

"My new neighbor." He sipped his beer. "She insisted on being my friend."

"Ha! I knew it." Jay rubbed his hands together gleefully.

"Stuff happened. You know. That's all."

"Define 'stuff.'"

Victor shook his head. "Look, this hasn't been going on for very long, and I have no idea where it's heading."

He just knew that he couldn't help smiling when he saw Amy's head pop up above the fence, and he got hard as a rock from thinking about her sitting in his lap.

"Tell me about her."

Victor sighed. "She inherited the house next door from her great aunt and is going to grad school. She's all sunshine and ladybugs and shit like that. Enjoys people and *talking*." What on earth she was doing with him, he had no idea.

Not that they were actually together; she was just making out with him every night. Maybe it meant nothing to her.

He didn't think that was true, though.

Across from him, Jay slapped the table and laughed. "I need to meet this woman. Let's go back to your place after this drink and you can invite her over."

"Nope, not happening."

"Fine, fine." Jay held up his hands in surrender. "But I'm happy for you, man."

"Uh, thanks."

The conversation moved on to other things, but even as Victor told Jay about his current project at work, his mind stayed on Amy.

~

It was nine o'clock and Victor was sitting in his backyard, waiting for Amy to appear. It would be foolish to pretend he was doing anything else. He wasn't even drinking something tonight. Nope, just staring out at the garden.

He wondered how her first day of grad school had gone.

"Hey, Victor!"

He startled.

She was right beside him, not on the other side of the fence.

"Sorry," she said. "I figured I might as well come right over. You were going to invite me over anyway, right?"

"If you hadn't invited yourself first, then yes."

She sat down next him and placed her hand on top of his.

"How was school today?" he asked.

"It was good! Not that I got much work done. I met my supervisor's other grad students, and one of them is showing me how to do things in the lab. On Thursday, I start my bridge design class."

"How many courses are you taking this term?"

"Two. I need to take five for my degree. I'm also TA-ing a course on reinforced concrete."

"Oh. That, um—"

"I know, it sounds thrilling! I have related work experience, so it shouldn't be too bad." She smiled. "I had lunch with one of the PhD students today. She knew a really great place for poke bowls. I'd never had one before."

It sounded just like Amy, already making friends, the way she'd insisted on making friends with him. At first he'd found her laugh annoying and her perkiness exhausting, but now here he was, waiting outside for her every night.

He'd come to rather like her chatter and her excitement. He wouldn't say it was infectious, not exactly…but okay, it did cheer him up the tiniest bit. She was a lovely distraction from his regular life, which he could admit was rather dull.

And she was an excellent kisser, and it felt so nice to have her pressed against him.

Amy climbed onto his lap and grinned down at him. She was wearing a dress again today, and God, there was so little between them.

"How was your day?" she asked.

"Not too bad." He paused. "I had drinks with a friend."

She gasped. "Look at you, being social."

He enjoyed her teasing.

"Don't expect it to happen again soon," he said. "Present company excepted, of course."

He slid his hands up her legs. Just to the tops of her knees—she hadn't given any indication she wanted more than that, but he was certain she'd tell him when she was ready.

She squirmed in his lap.

He'd be lying if he said he didn't jerk off every night, after she'd skipped back to her house. It never took long.

He wrapped his arms around her, one hand on the back of her head, and kissed her. It was hard to believe he had this—it didn't seem possible, after everything—but there it was.

She was so eager and affectionate with *him*. The mind boggled.

Sometimes he worried that if he blinked, he'd discover it was all a mirage.

When she moaned into his mouth and adjusted herself, it sent sparks shooting through him, and he kissed her even harder.

Eventually, her lips broke away from his, and she started kissing her way down his neck. Then she sat up straighter and shoved her breasts against his face.

"You know why I wore this dress today?" she asked. "Because it's low-cut, and it's easy for my breasts to pop free."

Well, that was a clear invitation. He slid his hand under the neckline, under her bra, and brushed his thumb over the peak of her nipple.

She gave the sweetest little gasp.

He freed her right breast, wishing he could spread her out naked on his bed, but this was pretty fucking great, too. He cupped the underside of her plump breast and raised the nipple to his mouth. When he ran his tongue around it and sucked it into his mouth, she gasped again, her hands tightening in his hair.

She just had one breast exposed. It would be explosive when he finally slid into her.

He slipped the straps of her dress and bra down her pretty shoulders—dusted with freckles—and bared both breasts.

"Yes?" he said.

She nodded, as though incapable of speech.

"Someone might see us out their window." He couldn't find it in him to be bothered by this, but she might feel differently.

"I don't care," she said. "Keep going."

He pressed her breasts together and nuzzled them, and then he drew the other nipple into his mouth. This one appeared to be even more sensitive than the first.

Oh, God.

He shifted beneath her, bringing her in closer contact with his erection. It was impossible to ignore how hard she was making him.

"Did you know my aunt Frances owned a store?" she asked.

It took him a moment to make sense of her words. Why was she telling him this now?

"No, I didn't," he said.

"A sex store." She was blushing. "I'd never owned a vibrator before, and I thought perhaps it was time. So I went there and got a very fancy one. I've been using it almost every day."

"Is that so?" he asked in a strangled voice. He was picturing it now. Amy lying on her bed, her skirt lifted, her underwear off…

"I usually think of you when I use it." She giggled and put a hand to her mouth.

"Usually?"

"The first time, I thought of a fictional character who looks a lot like you."

He chuckled as he shifted her hand away from her face—she seemed embarrassed that she'd told him this.

But she'd told him.

"I hope you don't mind that I think of you."

"Of course not," he murmured.

They made out for a few more minutes, and then Amy suddenly jumped up and righted her clothing. She was flushed and her hair was a little disheveled.

"I should go," she said.

"Okay."

"I'll see you tomorrow?"

"Tomorrow," he said.

She headed back to her house, and he was very, very certain that she was going to use her vibrator. God, he fucking ached for her. He wished he could watch.

Maybe one day…

[12]

AMY SIPPED her strawberry Earl Grey cider. Next to her, Sierra scarfed down Brussels sprouts.

They were at Ossington Cider Bar with Nicole, Charlotte, and Rose. Unfortunately, they were not sitting on the patio because it had been raining all day.

Amy was, frankly, crestfallen about the weather.

She couldn't expect Victor to wait outside for her in the rain.

It was silly to expect him to wait outside every night anyway. She should get his number.

Of course, she could just knock on his door tonight when she got home, but that seemed odd. It wasn't part of...whatever they'd been doing for the past week. She'd yet to step foot inside his house.

"What's new with you?" Nicole asked her.

It would be sensible for Amy to mention grad school, since it had started this week, but...

"She's been making out with our neighbor," Sierra answered for her.

Nicole's eyebrows rose. "Just making out?"

Amy sent a quick glare to Sierra, then changed it to a smile. She'd been planning to mention it anyway.

"Yeah, just kissing." *And sometimes he fondles my breasts.* "I want more, but my last relationship was a bad experience."

"What happened?" Rose asked. "If you want to tell us."

"I did so much for him, for us," Amy said, "and I never felt appreciated. When I finally dumped him, he was perplexed, couldn't see why I wanted anything different. I don't want to go through something like that again, and I've been enjoying my single life in Toronto."

Nicole nodded. "I know what you mean. When I was in a relationship, it felt like I lost part of who I was, and when I dumped his ass, it felt like I was taking back control. Finally getting to be myself again."

"Yeah, being in Toronto is about finding out who I am, without other people making lots of demands on my time."

"Then don't have a relationship. Just have sex with this guy."

Amy looked down. "I'm not sure if I can sleep with him when I know it's not going anywhere."

"Why not?" Sierra asked.

"I've been taught it's not what nice girls do." And it was hard to shake that mindset, even if she didn't believe it.

"Whatever," Nicole said. "Who cares about being *nice*?"

"I'm just…nice," Amy said. "People say that about me. I do what they ask. I'm the one who's always there to cheerfully help, no matter what."

Charlotte looked horrified. "That sounds like a nightmare."

"So don't do that," Nicole said. "Just have hot, sweaty sex. You'll both enjoy it—what's wrong with that? I've been single for eight years, but that doesn't mean I haven't gotten lots of action."

Amy had been told that women slept around because they had low self-esteem, but that wasn't Nicole. Granted, she didn't know Nicole very well, but she seemed pretty kick-ass. Taking what she wanted from life.

Why couldn't Amy be like that, too? The sexually-liberated city girl.

Besides, she'd gotten partially naked in his backyard the other night. She was already halfway there.

"What if it makes things more awkward between us?" she asked. "He lives next door. It's not like I can completely avoid him."

Nicole shrugged. "It'll only be awkward if you let it be awkward. Maybe this will turn into a friends-with-benefits situation. Since he's right next door, it's very convenient. You could be having sex a couple times a week."

Regular sex without any other expectations. Yeah, that did sound pretty awesome.

Amy wasn't used to such conversations about sex, but it was good to talk about these things with other women, rather than feeling like it was a dirty secret. She hadn't been sure what to do about Victor, but now she knew. She'd sleep with him a few times, get it out of her system... Or if not, it could become a regular thing.

She started guzzling her cider. "I'm, uh, feeling pretty tired after my first week of school. I think I'm going to head out and grab an Uber."

Sierra gave her a look. "Oh, really?"

"Yeah, you're not going home to bed," Nicole said. "At least, not alone."

"You got me." Why had Amy lied after the conversation they'd just had? Obviously her new friends knew exactly what she was doing. "Next time I'll stay longer, I promise."

For now, she wanted to get started on her new sexually-liberated self.

~

Not surprisingly, Victor wasn't in the backyard. It was still raining, after all.

So, Amy rang his doorbell. The last time she'd done this, she'd been bringing him a Tupperware of cookies, because she'd wanted to be his friend, and—

The door opened.

"Hi." Victor leaned on the doorframe.

God, he looked good. He was wearing blue gym shorts and a white T-shirt, pulled tight across his chest.

"I was out having cider with my new friends tonight!" she said cheerfully, even as her heart beat quickly in her chest. "But I left early."

"And why is that?" he asked.

"Because I wanted to see you."

"What did you want to do with me? Have a tea party?"

"Victor," she said, "don't be ridiculous."

He laughed softly. "Come in."

She slipped off her shoes and followed him into his living room. The room was neat and orderly. A couch, a recliner, a small table with a book. A large TV.

It looked nothing like Shane's living room.

Don't think about Shane.

Her ex had nothing to do with what she wanted from Victor.

He sat down on the couch and pulled her into his lap, as they'd done many times this week. But now, they were inside, and it was a little more comfortable.

He smoothed his hands over her waist and hips, and for a moment, they just stared at each other. Her rapid breaths were loud in the quiet room.

Then she bent down and kissed him as her hands slipped under his shirt.

Amy had done this much before, but tonight, she dragged his shirt over his head, gasping at the sight. She'd seen him shirtless before, but never up close. There were vines with flowers swirling over his right nipple, and on the left side, three Chinese characters and a profusion of cacti.

What did it say? What did it mean?

Perhaps she'd ask him…later. She traced a vine with her finger.

He hissed out a breath. "What would you like?"

"Tonight, I'm a confident, sexual woman, and I want *everything*."

She felt slightly unsure of herself now. It was weird being bold about stuff like this.

But his eyes darkened with desire. "You don't want to go home in half an hour and get yourself off with your vibrator?"

"No. I'd prefer to get off here. With you."

He stared at her, lips parted, as he slid his hands from her knees up her thighs. Farther than he'd gone before.

Not where she wanted him most.

When he slipped his finger under the edge of her panties, she started breathing even more quickly, but he didn't touch her *there*; instead, he kissed her, his tongue sweeping into her mouth. She kissed him back, squirming with need on his lap.

There was no reason to be ashamed. She felt good about this decision.

He inched his finger farther, to her entrance, just the barest brush of his slightly-callused finger against her sensitive skin.

She was very wet for him.

When he slid his finger inside, she let out a strangled cry.

He stilled, concentrating on her expression, as though everything he could want to know was written on her face. And perhaps it was.

She couldn't hide, and that was okay.

He moved his thumb to her clit.

Yes.

She started riding his finger, and his gaze bounced between her face and the juncture of her legs. She couldn't help raising one hand to her breast and running her thumb over her nipple through her clothing.

He growled and unbuttoned the first few buttons on her dress—how did he do that so smoothly with one hand? He shoved her clothing aside, and when he fastened his lips over her nipple, it was an overload of sensation. She kept riding his hand, faster and faster, swiveling her hips, until her orgasm overtook her and she collapsed against him.

Victor caressed her back as she stayed slack against his chest, then unbuttoned the rest of her dress. When he got to the last button, he shoved both sides apart and looked at her.

"I've had dreams about undoing all those buttons. About sticking my hand under your skirt and making you come." His voice was rough.

It was time to do one of the things *she'd* dreamed of.

She put her hands on his waistband. He lifted his hips, allowing her to slide his shorts and boxers partway down his thighs.

His cock popped free, erect.

She curled her hand around it and gave it an exploratory pump.

The hitch in his breathing sent pleasure curling through her. She loved that she made him so hard. She'd felt him in previous nights, through layers of clothing, but now she had her hand on him.

Her inner muscles clenched; she wanted to feel him inside her.

Amy reached into her purse and pulled out the condoms she'd bought on the way home. She ripped open a packet and handed it to him, since her hands were shaking too much. He rolled the condom on, his hands shaking, too, but somehow, he managed.

It felt like they were on the precipice of something important. Earth-shattering.

"You ready?" he asked.

She nodded jerkily, then raised herself up. She wrapped her hand around the base of his cock and eased herself down. He was thick and he filled her so good.

Oh, God, it was so good.

Her clothes were getting in the way. She shimmied out of her unbuttoned dress and tossed off her bra. His gaze dropped to her breasts, greedy, then up to her face.

And then he tenderly tucked a lock of hair behind her ear, and it was almost too much.

She started moving, bouncing up and down on his cock. Taking all the pleasure she could. She arched her chest toward him, and he buried his face in her breasts. His hard abs were right against her stomach; it was amazing to feel his skin against hers.

A week of kissing in his backyard, and now they were here. Joined.

He didn't speak, but she didn't need him to speak. Sure, he could have told her that she was sexy, but she felt sexy from the way he was touching her. He could tell her that he loved how wet she was for him, that being inside her felt fucking incredible, but she could see and feel it in everything he did, too.

Never had she felt like she could communicate so much without words.

He licked his thumb—and oh, it was hot to see his tongue peeking out of his mouth—before slipping his hand between her legs and circling her clit.

She rode him furiously, her fingers digging into his shoulders, her pleasure reaching up and up toward the peak...

It crashed over her, and she shuddered against him, losing her rhythm.

He pushed into her from below, again and again, until his breathing became louder and he emitted a low, long growl, holding her tightly against him.

She felt it all through her body as she clutched him, and then every muscle went into a state of complete relaxation.

"You good?" he murmured, his hand running over the perspiration on her forehead.

She'd had sex for the first time in almost a year. Just because she wanted sex, not because she hoped for anything more, and God, it had felt wonderful.

"Yes, I'm good," she said.

"Then let's get you into my bed."

~

Victor's room was on the third floor, the exact same room she had claimed in her house. She loved the sloping ceiling from the pointed roof of the house.

And she loved his king-sized bed.

He pulled off her panties—the only piece of clothing she was somehow still wearing—and then he flicked on the lights before laying her back on the bed and admiring her.

Amy was usually comfortable with her body, but the intensity with which he was studying her…

No, she would not be embarrassed. He clearly hadn't had his fill of her yet, even if his cock had softened between his legs. He was looking at her as though she was the most gorgeous thing he'd ever seen.

It was rather unnerving.

Especially when he was so gorgeous himself. She'd assumed he was tanned, but now she realized his skin was actually a little darker than she'd thought, because he was that color in places that probably never saw the sun, unless he went to the clothing-optional beach on the Toronto Islands.

His skin was a smooth, golden expanse, a beautiful canvas for his ink, and she wanted to explore every inch of him with her fingers and mouth.

And apparently, he felt the same way about her.

He pressed a kiss just under her jaw, then kept going downward, between her breasts, over the slight swell of her stomach, between her legs, and…*oh.*

He licked her entrance before sliding his tongue over her clit with just the right pressure, like he was already an expert on her body.

Though there was something else she wanted, too, and she'd ask for it and take all the pleasure she desired.

"Could you also touch me with your fingers?" Her voice was a bit squeaky.

He gave her a wicked look, then parted her folds with his thumbs and slid two fingers inside. She felt like she was going to shoot off the bed.

"Ohhh," she moaned.

He moved his fingers in and out of her as he continued licking her, and she found herself fisting the blankets and bucking her hips, and before she knew it, she was coming again.

Had she ever had this many orgasms in one night before?

She didn't think so.

He crawled up her body, predatory. His cock, now hard, bobbed between his legs.

"Can you take me again?" he asked.

"Yes. *Please.*"

That earned her a slight smile, and then he was rolling on another condom and pushing inside her.

He rocked his hips against hers, and as he fucked her, he ran one hand over her face and through her hair, a contrast of gentle and rough.

His powerful body seemed like it was built to please her.

She put a hand on the back of his head and pulled him down for a sloppy, inelegant kiss that felt like the best thing ever.

She didn't think she'd be able to come again, but as his breathing changed, her body answered with an orgasm of its own, and their cries mingled together.

He pulled out of her and pushed himself up to his hands and knees.

"Hey," he said. "How are you?"

Rather than powerful and virile, he seemed a touch vulnerable now.

"Good." She put her hands above her head and stretched. "Really good."

"You want to spend the night?"

Amy wasn't sure what Cool, Sexy City Girls did after they'd slept with their next-door neighbor. Her room was right on the other side of this wall; it would be easy to go home and curl up in her own bed.

Except she desperately wanted to stay, and if he was happy to have her, she'd take what she wanted because that was the kind of woman she was now.

"Yes," she said. "I'll stay."

Though he didn't smile, she could tell he was happy, like his happiness had been exuded from his pores and right into hers.

"I just need to text my roommate so she doesn't worry."

"I'll get your purse from downstairs," he said.

He cleaned himself up and when she heard the creak of the stairs, she headed to the washroom, which was easy to find since his house was the mirror image of hers. After washing her hands, she splashed water on her face and smiled at herself in the mirror. She looked flushed and satisfied and beautiful.

Yes, the whole casual sex thing was really agreeing with her.

Liar. What's casual about this?

She shoved her doubts aside and returned to the bedroom. She put on her underwear—it would feel weird to sleep without underwear—but nothing else. The rest of her clothes were downstairs anyway. Victor was already in bed, wearing only his boxers, and her purse was on the bedside table.

She sent Sierra a quick text, then turned off the sound and set her phone aside.

Now what? Would they snuggle? Or did he just want her to stay so he could have sex in the morning?

She couldn't help smiling when he answered her unspoken questions by wrapping his arms around her from behind.

"Goodnight, Amy," he murmured, kissing the back of her neck.

A minute later, he was asleep, and she was still in his arms.

She was rather disturbed by how much she enjoyed this.

[13]

W HEN V ICTOR WOKE up the next morning, there was a woman in his bed.

It had been a long time since this had happened.

The few times he'd slept with someone in the last several years, it had been at her place, not his, and he'd only stayed the night once.

But now Amy was here. Sleeping on her side, the blanket pushed down to her waist, exposing her breasts. She had one arm tucked under her head.

She looked lovely.

And he was afraid of what would happen when she woke up.

Last night, as they'd moved together in the shadows, he'd felt so close to her, his heart entwined with hers, but maybe it had been his imagination. Maybe she'd experienced nothing like that.

He was not used to such feelings. He usually kept himself separate, apart from it all. Perhaps these feelings were partly the result of not having sex for a long time.

But what frightened him the most was that she might regret it.

He expected she'd quickly cover her regret with a smile, so he had to see her face as soon as she awoke, before she had a chance to hide. He needed to know the truth.

Victor stared at the ceiling, his hands behind his head.

When he heard a rustle, he tilted his head toward Amy just as she opened her eyes.

There was no sign of regret in her expression. No surprise, either. She smiled at him as though this was the most natural thing in the world.

"Good morning," she said, her voice a bit husky.

She snuggled against his side, and he placed one hand on the curve of her hip and continued to look at the ceiling.

Why had he thought she'd regret it?

Amy seemed like the kind of person who was impulsive about little things. She might impulsively buy a ladybug mug or a vibrator, but many things in her life were well-planned. Take her move to Toronto, for example. Maybe he was flattering himself, thinking that he was more than a little thing, but they'd made out in his backyard for a week before they'd slept together. It hadn't come out of nowhere.

"Is something wrong?' she asked.

He turned to face her. "No, I just hadn't slept with anyone in a long time. I'm used to waking up alone."

Now she was the one searching his face for signs of regret, but he definitely didn't regret last night.

"It had been two years for me," he said.

"Two years?" She knit her brows in confusion. "Two years when you look like *this*?" She ran her hand over his abs.

He chuckled. "You may have noticed that I don't go out a lot."

"Yeah, you spend a lot of the time in your backyard. You'd probably do better if more women saw you cutting the grass without a shirt."

"I'll keep that in mind."

"There are apps."

"I know." He lifted a shoulder.

"So what you're saying is…" She rested a hand on his back. "I'm special."

Yes, you're special.

He couldn't manage to say that out loud. Instead, they simply looked at each other, and he didn't know if Amy was waiting for something, but he was waiting for her to say what she wanted. She was the sort of person who made such things clear.

It was another rainy day outside, and the only sound was the pitter-patter of the rain.

Her lips curved into a smile, and he found his own lips curving in response.

"Last night was pretty great, wasn't it?" she said.

He nodded.

She shifted herself on top of him. "What do you say we do that again?"

~

Amy perched on a stool in Victor's kitchen. She was wearing her dress from yesterday—wrinkled, because it had spent the night on the floor—and her make-up was smudged, but he still looked at her like she was gorgeous.

Yes, this had definitely been a good idea. Her body felt satisfied in a way it didn't from using her vibrator, as wonderful as that piece of equipment was.

She'd convinced Victor not to put on a shirt this morning, so he was walking around his kitchen shirtless while he prepared the French press and got out cereal, and she'd be lying if she said she wasn't enjoying the view.

"Are you sure you don't want me to cook something?" he asked as he set two boxes of cereal and a carton of soy milk in front of her. "An omelet?"

"No, this is good." For some reason, omelets seemed like a

relationship thing to her. Not what Cool City Girls Having Casual Sex ate with a man.

Or was she wrong about that? Maybe Cheerios suggested a level of comfort and intimacy with the other person.

Ugh. She didn't know what she was doing.

Perhaps she shouldn't be obsessing over breakfast food.

He placed the French press and two mugs on the counter and took a seat beside her. She poured some milk into her bowl then reached for the Cheerios.

"You pour your milk *before* your cereal?" he asked.

"Of course," she said. "It's the best way."

"Right."

"You sound skeptical."

"I am. You should pour your cereal in first like a proper person."

"Well," she said, poking his bicep, "I'm not a proper person. Neither are you. Your mug situation, for example, is decidedly improper."

"My mug situation?"

"Yes. All your mugs are plain blue."

"They came as a set."

"How awful! Why would you get plain mugs when there are so many exciting mugs out there? Donut mugs, llama mugs, ladybug mugs, sarcastic quote mugs…"

She was about to say she'd make it her mission to fix this horrible situation, but then she snapped her mouth shut. They were having friendly, neighborly sex, and buying him mugs seemed a bit intrusive.

But she couldn't deny that she enjoyed spending a lazy Sunday morning with him. The rain beat on the roof, but inside, they were warm and cozy and *together*.

Yeah, she didn't feel like a Cool City Girl Having Casual Sex.

∼

When Amy got home—it was so convenient to spend the night with someone who lived next door—she had a shower, then checked her phone for the first time since last night.

It was almost eleven thirty. Wow. She was usually an earlier riser, even on the weekend, and would typically have gotten quite a bit done by eleven thirty.

She had a bunch of messages and missed calls, so she set about taking care of those.

So, did you do it? Nicole asked.

Well, that was easy to answer.

Yes!! And it was awesome.

She'd also had calls from her parents and both of her brothers. On any other day of the week, the fact that everyone in her family had tried to contact her in a short period of time might have worried her, but Sunday morning was a favorite for phone calls in her family.

She headed to the reading room, snuggled up by the window, and called her parents.

"Hi, Amy," Mom said. "Where were you earlier?"

"Sorry, I was in the shower."

"At ten in the morning? That isn't like you."

Yeah, actually, I was banging the guy next door.

Nope, her family wasn't going to know the details of her life in Toronto.

"Got up a little late today," she said.

She couldn't help the guilt that pierced through her. She didn't like lying to people, and she'd done something her mother would not approve of. Mom had always been clear that sex was for marriage, or at least for long-term relationships. It wasn't something to be taken lightly.

But there was nothing wrong with what she'd done.

"How was your first week of grad school?" Mom asked. "Exhausting? Is that why you slept in?"

They talked for a few minutes, and then Amy called Fred.

"Hi, Amy," Fred said. There was some commotion in the background. "I'm putting you on speakerphone. The girls want to sing you a song."

"No, just me!" Abigail cried. "I want to sing the song myself. Mellie screws it up every time. She's cramping my style."

Amy couldn't help laughing.

A brief argument ensued, and somehow the outcome was that Jessie and Mellie—four-year-old twins—would sing Amy "Happy Birthday," even though it wasn't her birthday.

After an adorable off-tune rendition of "Happy Birthday," it was Abigail's turn. She went with a Christmas song, unbothered by the fact that Christmas was more than three months away.

Amy winced when she realized her niece was singing "The Twelve Days of Christmas." It was far from a short song, but she didn't protest, and she complimented Abigail on getting the lyrics right.

"Did you get my drawing in the mail?" Abigail asked earnestly after finishing the song. "Did you like it?"

"Of course I loved it. And you did a very good job at addressing the envelope."

It was misdelivered, but fortunately my neighbor brought it over.

Amy had gotten it over a week ago, but she hadn't bothered to tell Abigail. She'd been too absorbed with her life in the city, too busy with Victor.

She talked to Fred for a few minutes, and after she ended the call, she felt an uncomfortable stirring in her chest. She did miss her family. Maybe she should have gone to Silver River for Labor Day weekend. She hadn't wanted to go back right before school started, but Thanksgiving was still a month away.

Lastly, she called her other brother, Steven. He was two years older than her and lived in Sudbury. Although she'd sent him a few texts, he hadn't replied, so she was pleased he'd called. Things had been rather tense between them for several months, since he'd been upset that she'd inherited the house.

Unfortunately, when she returned his call, it went right to voicemail.

But she wasn't too bothered. She'd had great sex last night and this morning. Despite the weather, it felt like there was sunshine flowing through her veins.

She should really do this sex business more often.

If she and Victor were going to have a friends-with-benefits arrangement, when should she knock on his door next? Would tonight be too soon? Should she wait for next weekend?

Well, she wouldn't worry about it now. Maybe she'd ask Sierra or Nicole for advice later.

This afternoon, she'd do her Sunday chores...and whistle while she cleaned.

~

No matter what Amy did that day—laundry, vacuuming, scrubbing the tub—she kept thinking about Victor.

The way his hand had brushed hers when he passed her a mug of coffee. The way he'd teased her about her cereal and milk—there was nothing wrong with pouring the milk before the cereal, thank you very much.

The way his eyes had looked almost pleading when he'd asked her to stay the night. The way he'd pushed inside her. The way he'd focused on her, and only her.

She also thought about him doing various things shirtless. Like cutting the grass and making coffee, but also lifting weights and lifting her and...

Fine, yes, she had fantasies about him using his muscles to lift things.

And taking her to the movies and out for drinks.

He'd never told her what he wanted, but Amy had set out to have no-strings-attached sex, and now she couldn't deny that she wanted something more.

Was she simply bad at casual sex? Did she not have Nicole's skill?

Or was it Victor? Could she have managed no-strings-attached sex with someone else, just not with him?

There had been *feelings* involved last night. Nascent feelings, but still.

Yeah, her plan wasn't going to work.

When she'd moved to Toronto—just over a month ago now—her plan had been to focus on herself and her new life. No dating.

But she'd also vowed to go after what she wanted in life.

And so that was what Amy Sharpe would do: she'd ask for more, because that was what she wanted now.

She wouldn't deny that it was scary. Maybe Victor just wanted sex, nothing more, with a Cool City Girl. The only time she'd asked a guy out, back before she'd met Shane, she'd been shot down. He'd laughed at her, in fact, and she'd been so embarrassed.

What would Victor say?

～

The next night, Amy made two batches of chocolate chip cookies. One for Sierra, and one for Victor.

She put on her sunflower dress, which looked cute and made her feel brave, and headed to Victor's. She rang the doorbell, and it didn't take him long to answer.

Did his eyes light up when he saw her, or was that her imagination?

She hoped it wasn't her imagination.

"Hey, Amy," he said.

"Hi! I brought you cookies." She thrust them in his direction.

"I feel like I'm having déjà vu. Aren't we beyond a neighborly batch of cookies now?"

"Who doesn't like cookies? I'll take them back if you don't want them."

He plucked the container out of her hands. "What's up?"

She launched into her speech, her heart thumping fast. "You see, I'd thought we could have casual neighborly sex like cool city people and that was my intention Saturday night when I knocked on your door. I was out with some friends and they convinced me and…yeah. I thought it would be fun, and it *was* fun, but now, I'm thinking I want to go on a date with you?"

"Ah. I see."

What did that mean? Did he want what she did?

"I hadn't planned to date this year," she said, "after what happened with Shane. I mean, I was with him for a while and we broke up near the end of last year, so it hasn't been that long and—"

"Yes," Victor said.

"Yes?"

"I'll go on a date with you."

She clapped her hands as warmth spread through her. He wanted this, too!

"Excellent! I'll plan something. This Friday?"

"Sure, that works."

"Great. Well, I should be off now."

"Amy." His hand wrapped around hers before she could hop off the porch. "Would you like to come in for some chocolate chip cookies? I just received a whole container."

"Cookies? Maybe with tea? How wholesome."

"There won't be anything wholesome about the way I feed them to you."

Oh.

Oh.

He pulled her inside, and later that evening…

Well, she'd never look at a chocolate chip cookie the same way again.

[14]

IF ONLY CHRISTIAN could see him now.

Except Victor's life had been different when his brother had been alive. He'd always been a bit of an introvert who'd never gone out as much as his younger brother, but he'd been more social back then. Dated a bit. So this wouldn't have seemed as out of character as it felt now.

He rang Amy's doorbell. He was wearing a navy suit, no tie. She'd told him to dress up a little, and he hoped he hadn't screwed this up.

When she appeared at the door, she took his breath away.

She was wearing a dress, which wasn't unusual for her, but today she was wearing heels with it. And the dress...*oh*. It was a thing of beauty on her. It was made of some kind of flowy pink material, and it clung to her curves. When she turned to get her purse, he noticed the bow on the back.

He swallowed. "Uh. You look nice."

Why did he sound uncertain? He wasn't uncertain at all about her looking nice.

"You, too." She grinned. She looked super excited, like she

expected to have the best night of her life, and he didn't want to disappoint her.

"Where are we going?" he asked.

"A restaurant in Yorkville."

"Which one?"

"You'll see. You up for walking?"

"Sure, if you can walk in those." He looked at her silver high-heeled shoes.

"Don't worry about me. I'll manage."

They headed down to the sidewalk. Should he hold her hand? Or was holding hands not the sort of thing you did on a first date? He had no idea.

Yes, it was a first date, but they'd already slept together several times. After she'd shown up at his door with cookies on Monday, they'd finally exchanged phone numbers. They'd texted a bunch of times during the week and had sex each day.

Wow. Look at him. Out on a date. Smiling. Sort of.

Was this real life?

He bent his arm and offered it to her, and she wrapped her hand around it.

They arrived at the restaurant twenty-five minutes later. It was a small-plates Middle Eastern restaurant called Mosaic, and Amy beamed at the hostess as she led them to a table on the rooftop patio.

"I wanted to go to this place because of the patio," Amy said as she opened her menu.

"Not for the food?" he asked.

"The food is supposed to be very good, but I thought the rooftop patio would make it very date-ish." She looked around. "Look at all the fancy people! I called for a reservation on Wednesday, and I lucked out because they had a cancelation—I didn't know you needed to make reservations so far in advance." She held out the drink menu. "The cocktails are supposed to be really good, but we can have wine if you want, and there's also an extensive scotch selection. I checked."

"It's great." It was hard to believe someone had gone to all this effort for *him*. Why, the first couple times he'd seen her, all he'd done was give her a curt nod.

And then she'd barreled into his life, and here they were.

Yeah, Christian would definitely laugh.

Victor's jacket felt uncomfortably warm and restricting. He had to wear suits sometimes for business meetings, but he was never at ease in them. He took off his jacket and draped it over the back of his chair, then rolled up the sleeves of his shirt.

Amy's gaze immediately latched onto his forearms.

This place was far too public for what he wanted to do. He'd push up her dress, bend her over the table, and then—

"Can I get you started with something to drink?" A waitress appeared next to the table.

"I'll, uh, have a Manhattan," he said.

"We have a list of special Manhattans." The waitress opened his menu. "Twists on the classic, if you'd like to try one."

Oh, geez. Why were there so many choices?

He pointed to one that claimed to have smoked maple syrup.

Amy, on the other hand, was not at all flustered and quickly gave the waitress her order. She'd probably picked out everything she wanted to try beforehand.

It was unfair that his brain had to function, even in a limited capacity, when she looked like that. Her lipstick was bright pink today, and her eye make-up seemed a little heavier than usual. Her hair was up in some kind of style that looked more effortless than it likely was.

She was more beautiful than any other woman here.

Not that he'd taken a look around, but he knew it all the same.

And she was with him.

Under the table, he placed his hand on her knee and slid it upward.

"Victor!" She giggled. "Later. We have to figure out what to order first."

They decided on lamb ribs, labneh, artichoke salad, marinated octopus, and rice pilaf. The sight of Amy enjoying her food was almost unbearably sensual. They both picked up their lamb ribs to eat them—because the ribs seemed impossible to eat with a knife and fork—and it felt like a faux pas at a nice restaurant, but he enjoyed watching her put the rib to her mouth.

They were just about finished their food when Victor noticed Amy looking at his near-empty cocktail glass.

"You want a sip?" he asked. "It's mostly melted ice cubes now, but—"

"Actually, I was wondering if I could have your cherry."

She laughed after she said it, and he found himself laughing with her.

"Of course." He didn't like these maraschino cherries anyway —they were overly sweet. He'd always thought they were kind of stupid, to be honest, but as Amy lifted it to her lips...

Well, his suit pants felt rather tight.

Amy refused dessert, declaring she had other plans, and when the waitress brought over the bill, Victor whisked it away before Amy could reach for it.

"You paid for dim sum," she said. "I'll pay for this."

"This is much more expensive than dim sum."

"I invited you out. I'll pay."

"You're a student. It's fine, I promise."

"I inherited a house in Toronto. I'm in a good place financially."

He should probably tell her.

"I'm actually quite well-off. I could afford to buy my house a few times over." It was awkward to talk about this, but he didn't want her thinking it was a hardship for him to pay on a date.

"I thought you were a software developer. What have you been hiding from me?"

"I *am* a software developer. My brother and I started a company, and it's doing pretty well. He once said that I'm the brains and he's the charm."

Victor used to be more involved in running the company, but after his brother's death, he'd wanted to step back. So he did mostly software development these days, yes.

But he wasn't comfortable saying any more about his brother yet.

"That's cool," Amy said. "You can pay, if you insist. As long as you let me pay for gelato."

"Sure." It seemed important to her to pay for something, so he'd let her. "We're having gelato for dessert?"

"You may not have noticed, but I love ice cream and gelato, and there are so many exciting things to try in Toronto."

She took him to a nearby chocolatier. There were ten flavors of gelato, all hidden from view in metal containers. Amy got boozy cherry chocolate—he'd known she would get this as soon as he saw it—and bananas foster. He ordered Mayan dark chocolate, figuring he'd get something with chocolate since it was a chocolate shop, and passionfruit.

As promised, he let her pay.

Amy worried her bottom lip as she looked around. The shop had limited seating, and it was full.

"I know where we can sit," he said.

It was only a two-minute walk to the giant rock on Cumberland. The piece of the Canadian Shield had been carted to Toronto, probably at great expense. There were several people already sitting on it, enjoying the late summer night. Autumn would officially be here in a week.

"Oh, I love it!" Amy said, and her delight—even though it wasn't an uncommon thing—warmed something inside him. She sat down on the rock, and he sat next to her. His suit pants would get a little dirty, but that was okay.

His leg pressed against hers as he watched her slide that tiny spoon of gelato into her mouth, and it nearly undid him. When he finally remembered to eat his own gelato, he discovered it was pretty freaking amazing.

"Want to try some of mine?" Amy held a spoonful of boozy cherry chocolate up to his mouth, and he closed his lips over the spoon.

"It's good." But even if it had been an artificial-tasting vanilla gelato, he would have said the same thing. All he cared about was being here beside her.

He felt like a lucky fucking bastard.

Amy was definitely pleased with her decision to ask Victor on a date. She'd forgotten how fun this dating business could be.

Though she'd never been on a date as fun as this one before, even if most people probably wouldn't think of Victor as a *fun* guy.

Yeah, she definitely needed to go on more dates.

But there was no denying that she only wanted to go on dates with one particular man. My God, he looked amazing in that suit.

Well, he'd forsaken the jacket a long time ago, but she appreciated seeing the sleeves of his shirt rolled up.

When she shivered—the night was cooler than she'd expected—he draped the jacket over her shoulders, and she hugged it around herself, wanting to breathe in more of his scent.

She loved this rock. It reminded her of the rock she used to sit on back in Silver River. She'd go there just to be alone and dream.

In a way, this moment felt like her past and future colliding. Everything she wanted, everything she'd been and would be…

Somehow, this moment perfectly contained all of it.

She set aside her empty gelato cup and wrapped her arms

around Victor's waist. He leaned into her and kissed her forehead, and she smiled into the night.

Yep. Perfection.

Could something like this last?

Tonight, she couldn't help believing it with all her heart.

[15]

Victor had knocked on Amy's door at six o'clock last night, and it was now two in the afternoon the following day.

They'd been together for twenty straight hours.

True, about eight of those hours had been sleep—okay, seven, given what had happened at three in the morning—but still. It was a lot of time to spend with a person.

In fact, it was impressive that he'd managed to spend so much time with Amy and not feel like he was going completely out of his mind.

And *that* scared him.

Some time alone would do him good.

"So, what would you like to do now?" Amy asked. She was partially reclined on the couch, her legs in his lap.

"Actually, I'd…" He briefly considered saying he had work to do, but he didn't feel like lying. He wouldn't tell her everything, though. "I need a little time alone. To recharge. I'm used to spending most of my time, outside of work, by myself."

Her smile never faltered as she swung her feet to the ground. "Of course! I totally understand. I have things to do, too."

Yeah, she was great.

He was a lucky fucking bastard indeed.

He kissed her goodbye, then he made himself some coffee, went up to the second floor, and sank onto a chair in the sunroom. He'd spent most of the past five years alone in this house.

His brother's house.

Victor had lived in a condo, but it had been important to Christian to own a house with a yard, and so he'd bought this place when their company started doing well, a few years before he died.

Once he was gone, no one had wanted to sell the house he'd loved, least of all Victor.

The first six months had been hell. Full of unbearable pain he couldn't ease. He liked being able to fix things. But nothing would bring his brother back.

Sometimes, he wouldn't sleep for days.

Once, he'd been washing dishes, and he'd gotten frustrated at a piece of food that wouldn't come off—he'd forgotten to rinse his bowl after using it. He'd chucked the bowl against the wall, the wall he'd helped his brother paint, and it had shattered.

Which wasn't like him at all.

So he'd made himself numb. That was the only way to go on. To manage.

Victor had kept his life small and ordered for years, and now, Amy was turning it upside down, making him do ridiculous shit like going out for gelato and having fun. Spending the morning in bed snuggling.

He didn't want to pull back from her. He wanted to keep seeing her. She wanted more than just sex, and he liked that idea, too. She made him smile, and it had been a damn long time since he'd had anyone like her in his life.

But now that he'd spent twenty freaking hours with her and admitted to himself just how much she was disrupting his carefully-controlled world…well, these burgeoning feelings in his chest weren't exactly comfortable. He sipped his coffee and stared at the cacti. One of them had died a couple years ago, and he'd been furious with himself for killing a fucking cactus. He'd immediately gone out and purchased another of the same kind.

He'd show Amy this room, one day soon. Tell her about his brother. Amy, who'd never known the *before* in his life, who didn't know who he used to be.

He felt an urge to tell her things.

And it seemed totally unfair that she could never meet Christian.

Dear God, what was happening to him?

And when would he see her again? What would she want to do together next?

~

Amy was in a great mood.

She did a load of laundry and even folded her clothes right away. She went grocery shopping and cleaned.

And it was all effortless. Because she just felt so good.

Victor had wanted some time to himself, and yes, that had disappointed her a little. But from what she knew of him—he wasn't an extrovert like her—it was perfectly understandable, and he'd given her a scorching goodbye kiss.

At eight that evening, Amy was making herself some tea when Sierra came home.

Sierra walked into the kitchen and set a red tin on the table. "How was your date last night? I didn't see you this morning, so I assume it was good?"

"Yes." Amy sighed dreamily, unable to help it. "The best."

"I'm glad," Sierra said. "I bought mooncakes for the Mid-Autumn Festival. You want to try some?" She lifted up the lid on the tin, revealing four cakes with intricate designs on the top, each in its own little package.

Amy lifted one up. It was heavier than she'd expected.

"They're pretty dense," Sierra said. "Two are lotus, and two are red bean. Which do you want to try first?"

"The lotus," Amy said, recalling the sesame balls she'd enjoyed at dim sum.

Sierra removed one of the mooncakes from the package and cut it into quarters. "There's salted egg inside. I think it's supposed to represent the moon."

Amy made some tea for Sierra, then took a small bite of mooncake.

"What do you think?" Sierra asked.

"It's really good, and I like the egg. It's different."

Sierra smiled at her. "You look radiant. Even more so than usual. The beginning of a relationship is always the best. I remember what that was like with Justin."

"Justin?"

"My ex-husband. The first month was so exciting. Finding someone who seemed to get me, who wanted the same things. I'd never had that before. The sex was great, too, I won't lie."

"What happened? What did he do?"

"He didn't do anything. It just faded, and we were left with a comfortable, passion-less marriage, which isn't exactly comfortable after a while."

"But the beginning was good?"

"Yeah. Though to be honest, it was my first relationship, so I had nothing to compare it to. I'm sure that's not the case for you."

No, Amy had had a few relationships.

None of those had been as wonderful as this.

Still, Sierra's words made her doubt herself. Maybe thinking it could stay this wonderful was foolish.

But then she thought of Victor and couldn't help smiling.

~

The next morning, Amy went to Harbord Coffee Bar.

Lucy was working, and they chatted briefly about the weather —and the new black sesame roll cake on the menu—before Amy ordered her latte and brought it to a table by the window. This was her favorite spot, so she could watch the passersby when she wasn't reading.

She had the first Sierra Wu book with her today. Her copy was well-worn; she re-read it every year. But this time, re-reading it was different from usual.

Because her housemate was named Sierra Wu, which was slightly disorienting.

And she was dating a guy who looked a bit like Rebel.

In fact, the first time Rebel appeared on the page, Amy got lost in her thoughts of Victor, remembering how he'd kissed his way down her body yesterday morning.

She hadn't gone to see him last night. She'd been slightly unsettled after what Sierra had said and figured she'd give him some space.

She fully intended to see him today, though, and maybe suggest a fun midweek date. Perhaps she could visit Sierra's shop and get him a cute card or mug.

But then she started worrying.

Shane had only bought her a card once. She loved cards, and she'd made it clear that she would appreciate the occasional card, but all she'd gotten was a single birthday card with a stupid joke. She'd loved it anyway.

Amy couldn't deny that in some ways, her relationship with Victor seemed to be following the same path as her relationship with Shane.

She was the one planning the dates.

She was the one making all the effort.

That's how it had been from the beginning. She'd brought him cookies and tried to be friends with him. When he'd knocked on her door to deliver a letter, she'd been ecstatic and asked him out for a friendly lunch.

Relax, you've only been on one real date. He clearly likes you a lot.

Yeah, she didn't doubt he was interested.

She just didn't want to end up in another one-sided relationship.

Was it so wrong to want a man who occasionally gave her cards and flowers? A man who asked her on a date sometimes, rather than the other way?

She'd spent a lot of her life giving. Doing things for other people. Being taken for granted, because she was good at organizing and saying "yes."

She'd never had trouble taking initiative when it came to little things. *Hey, you want to meet up for dinner?* But she hadn't been good at making the life she wanted for herself.

Until this year, when she'd moved to Toronto, even though it had made her family unhappy.

Amy wouldn't let Victor turn her back to her old ways.

No, she'd tell him what she needed. What she deserved.

The idea of having that conversation made her uncomfortable —a hell of a lot more than uncomfortable, in fact.

She took a deep breath. She'd work herself up to it.

Tomorrow, perhaps.

Monday evening, Victor paced his hallway.

He'd sat on his patio for hours yesterday, but Amy had never emerged. He'd sat there again after work today. Still no Amy.

He hadn't seen her since Saturday afternoon, when he'd asked her to leave so he could have some time alone.

Now, he regretted it.

Had she taken it the wrong way? Why didn't she want to see him?

True, it had only been two days, but she lived next door, and they usually saw each other every day. He'd thought she would have appeared by now. Texted him at the very least. Asked him to go to a hipster coffee shop with her.

Should he cut the grass without a shirt? Would that bring her out of hiding?

And then it hit him.

Why couldn't *he* plan something?

Sure, he'd sat in his backyard to wait for her every night, but he'd let her make all the effort. Maybe she thought he "wasn't that into her" or whatever the hell it was. Hadn't there been a book by that title? Or a movie, perhaps?

But he was definitely into her.

He was so into her that he thought about her every morning when he woke up, and every night before he fell asleep. And many, many times in between.

He was so into her that it made him uncomfortably off-balance.

He smacked his forehead. *Of course.*

She'd told him about her last relationship, about how she'd done all the work and planned everything. She didn't want that anymore.

Amy needed to be appreciated.

Amy needed someone to do something just for her.

Sure, she was a little goofy and obsessed with rainbow sprinkles and such, but she came across as so competent, the person you counted on to have great ideas and get things done. A guy could feel like he was along for the ride when he was with her.

But she didn't have to do it all herself. He didn't *want* her to do it all herself. He wanted to look after her.

Victor felt a slight discomfort at the thought, but it was overwhelmed by his excitement—oh, God, he was actually excited!—because he knew what she needed, and he could give it to her.

He went to his laptop and started doing some research.

~

As soon as Victor rang her doorbell, he wondered if this was a bad idea.

No, the date was definitely a good idea, but it was nearly ten o'clock at night, and perhaps it was too late. But he would prefer to ask her in person and hadn't wanted to wait, even though he was usually a patient guy.

Amy answered the door, looking cute in pajama pants and a T-shirt.

"Hi, Victor," she said.

"Uh, hi." He scratched the back of his neck. He was nearly forty years old; he should not have difficulty asking out a woman, especially when they'd already slept together and shared a nice dinner. "I was wondering if you'd like to go out with me on Friday."

"Where would we go?"

"Don't worry, I have it all planned out." He tried to sound breezy, but breezy was not something he did well. "Dinner, drinks, dessert."

"Oh!" She clapped her hands and practically squealed with delight, and it made his heart fucking sing. "What should I wear?"

"Just something comfortable for walking. You don't need to dress up."

"I accept." She paused. "Friday, you say? I can wait that long for a date, but I don't think I can wait that long for...other things." She raised her eyebrows.

Not two minutes later, they were in his bed.

[16]

AMY HAD BEEN THINKING about what she wanted from Victor, trying to work up the courage to tell him, and then he'd shown up at her door and invited her on a date! How cool was that?

She was very much looking forward to Friday's date, but she was looking forward to tonight, too. She and Sierra were going to a new burger place on College Street. Part of the reason Amy wanted to go was because their Instagram made her drool, and the reviews were also pretty good.

She met Sierra at the burger place after her roommate had closed up Moonbeam Messages for the day. It had been quite nice earlier, but now the clouds were rolling in, and Amy wondered if she should have brought her ladybug umbrella.

Oh, well. Hopefully it wouldn't be raining once they finished dinner.

They both studied the menu at the counter. There were ten burgers, and all of them looked delicious to Amy. Literally, all of them. There were things she'd never had before on burgers, like blue cheese, mushrooms, caramelized onions, and tzatziki. Eventually, she settled on sweet potato fries and the burger with blue cheese and sautéed mushrooms. It was more than twice as expensive as burgers at the Silver River Diner, but she was sure it would be worth it.

The burger joint was small. Amy and Sierra squeezed into the only table available, next to a couple who were arguing about how to eat burgers. The woman ate her burgers upside down, and the man insisted that this was wrong. Not in a friendly teasing sort of way; no, he seemed truly offended by it.

"So, how was your day?" Amy asked Sierra.

"Not too bad, but it was a little slow at the store. Aside from the woman who came in and bought all the cards with unicorns."

"How many unicorn cards do you have?"

"Four. Three birthday cards and one that's blank inside." Sierra sighed. "My attempts at using dating apps aren't going well, either."

"Oh, you started that?"

"You sound surprised."

"You told me you were going to, but…" Amy paused. "Just the way you were talking about the beginning of relationships the other day. As though you didn't believe love could last."

"I'm not sure what I believe anymore, but maybe it's worth a try. Unfortunately, I chose an app that wants you to use your real name, and in addition to the regular creepy messages, one guy sent a screenshot of the sex scene in the first Sierra Wu book and asked if I'd do that. Another guy had a super disturbing Asian fetish. Anyway, I've already deleted the app."

"Ugh." Amy made a face. "That sounds awful. But you'll find someone. I'm positive."

"Sometimes you sound like a unicorn greeting card," Sierra muttered, but she said this much more kindly than the man critiquing his partner's burger-eating. "I wish I could be that way. I don't know, maybe I need a little longer before I get back in the game."

"And who knows, perhaps someone will run into you with a

durian ice cream cone from Ginger Scoops. Wouldn't that be a cute way to meet a man?"

"A stinky way."

Amy laughed.

Their burgers came a few minutes later. Amy tried a sweet potato fry first. Mmm, those sure were good. Perhaps she could find a recipe and make them at home.

Before trying her burger, she took a picture for her Instagram. It didn't look quite as impressive as the restaurant's Instagram feed, but she was sure it would taste delicious.

Amy bit into her burger…

And to her disappointment, it was just okay.

She'd had blue cheese before, but only on salads, and now discovered she wasn't a fan of it on a burger. The mushrooms were good, though. The burger itself…

Well, it was comparable to the burgers at the Silver River Diner. Not bad, but not worth the price.

"How's your burger?" she asked Sierra.

"It's okay, but the ones at the cider bar are better. I feel misled by the Yelp reviews."

Amy tried not to dwell on it. The sweet potato fries were still delicious, and she couldn't expect everything she ate in Toronto to be the best thing ever, right?

Besides, she was here with her friend.

And a loud couple arguing right next to them.

Victor would never get angry at her for how she ate her burger, would he? Sure, he'd teased her about pouring her milk before her cereal, but that was different.

Amy ate her burger upside down in solidarity with the woman beside her, even though she probably wouldn't notice.

"I liked your chicken casserole more than this," Sierra whispered to Amy.

"I feel the same way about the noodles you made on Sunday."

They both smiled.

When they were finished their dinner, they headed to the door and discovered it was pouring rain—there were no windows at the back, and they hadn't heard it over the commotion. Two customers entered the burger joint, utterly soaked. Amy wished she'd brought her umbrella, then noticed how strong the wind was. No, her cute ladybug umbrella wouldn't have done much good in this weather.

"You want to make a run for it?" Sierra asked.

"We're not that close to home."

"But we're three doors down from a bubble tea shop."

They ran, laughing, through the rain, and were wet—not soaked, but close—when they arrived, even though it wasn't far at all. It was really coming down out there.

Amy ordered a taro milk tea, and when she sucked the first tapioca pearl up the straw, she managed to choke on it.

"You okay?" Sierra asked.

Amy nodded but kept coughing.

When she recovered, she looked suspiciously at the tapioca pearls—they were like oversized blueberries to her—in the bottom of her cup.

The taro milk tea was good, but the passionfruit green tea she'd had last time had been slightly better. Taro, she decided, was better in ice cream form.

Then again, most things were best in ice cream form, weren't they?

The tea shop was small, like the burger joint—though both were still bigger than XLB. Amy wondered how much the rent would be on a place like this in downtown Toronto. Probably far from cheap.

They took their time drinking their bubble tea, but when they left, it was still pouring.

As they hurried back to their house, they passed an empty unit with a lovely mural of cherry blossoms on the side. Unfortunately, someone had spray-painted "fuck climate change deniers" over it, and though Amy agreed with the sentiment, the mural would have looked better without it. They also passed a garbage can overflowing with wet trash. And was that a rat nosing around in there?

Amy felt like she was noticing everything that wasn't quite perfect today, and when she and Sierra headed up the walkway to their house, she was in a slightly odd mood.

Still, she couldn't help smiling when she looked at the house next to hers.

"You going to visit Victor?" Sierra asked.

"Yeah, I think I will."

Sierra winked at her. "I won't expect you home tonight."

Victor opened the door almost immediately, and Amy's cold, wet skin started tingling.

"Let's get you out of those clothes and warm you up," he said as he led her inside and shut the door. "No umbrella or polka dot boots today?"

"I didn't realize it was supposed to rain."

He started peeling off her shirt, and she kissed his warm, dry skin.

And as she held him close, she felt like even if things weren't perfect, they were pretty damn great.

[17]

AFTER GETTING home on Friday afternoon, Amy prepared for her date. She tried on various outfits and finally settled on a pair of dark jeans with a black off-the-shoulder shirt and two long necklaces.

The doorbell rang promptly at five thirty—it was easy to be right on time when the trip over was so predictable, haha—and she scurried to the door.

Victor was leaning against the doorframe, wearing jeans and a casual striped button-down shirt with the sleeves rolled up, looking delicious as always.

She smiled at him, put on her shoes, and threw a cardigan in her purse—the nights were getting cooler now. Luckily, the forecast said there was a zero percent chance of precipitation.

"Where are we going?" she asked as they started walking north. "Will you tell me now?"

"All I'm saying is that we're having dessert first."

"Dessert first? How shocking!"

"I know. I'm usually just so well-behaved."

She snorted.

"What?" he said, casually shoving his hands in his pockets.

"Do you need to be reminded of what we did last night?"

"No." He leaned down and whispered, "I can't wait to get you out of those jeans."

Yeah, she couldn't wait for that, either. She was insatiable around him, and today she'd brought something special in her purse for when they got back to his place.

She was slightly nervous at the thought, to be honest.

She swallowed and lifted his hand from his pocket. "Your tattoos are hardly the mark of a *well-behaved* man."

"Tattoos are common. Besides, look at all the foliage on my arm. Vines? Flowers? It's practically cross-stitching. I'm like a grandmother."

She snorted again. When she'd first met Victor, she hadn't imagined him being playful, but she enjoyed this side of him.

They arrived at their destination: A Cup of Stars.

"It closes at seven. That's why we had to come before dinner," he explained.

"Have you been here before?"

"No. I picked it just for you."

Warmth slid through her as he opened the door and they stepped inside. There was a wide array of baked goods, including large scones and brownies.

"Should we get our own, or should we share?" she asked.

"I think we should share. Dinner will be pretty big."

She chose a brownie and ordered a latte as well. She didn't usually have espresso after five, but she really wanted a latte. Besides, she had a feeling she'd be happy to stay up late with Victor.

She walked toward a table by the window, but he placed a hand on her arm.

"Let's check out the backyard patio."

A backyard patio? How awesome. He was the amazing-est at planning dates.

She carried the brownie, and he carried their mugs to the patio.

It was, in a word, enchanting.

Among the patio furniture, there were potted plants, even a few roses growing up a trellis. And then there were the murals. The one on the building to the right was of a little girl looking up at a starry night sky. The kind of starry night Amy couldn't see in Toronto, but it reminded her of Silver River. On the other building, there were close-ups of roses and sunflowers. Unlike the mural she'd seen with Sierra, these ones hadn't been vandalized.

Amy grinned at Victor and sat down at a table.

"It's wonderful," she said. "I love it."

The brownie was deliciously moist and chocolatey. It was definitely the best brownie she'd ever eaten, or was that partly because she was here with Victor, in this little garden oasis?

Before they left, she sent a quick text to Charlotte, telling her about this place. Although Charlotte didn't go out a lot, she was a hardcore caffeine addict who enjoyed a good latte.

Amy and Victor continued walking until he stopped outside a restaurant on Bloor, its large windows open to let in the night air.

"It smells like sausage," she said, her stomach rumbling.

"It's a German-style beer hall."

Inside, most of the patrons were seated at what looked like long picnic tables, but the hostess showed them to a table for two at the back.

"Is this okay?" Victor asked as the hostess left them with their menus. "The food is supposed to be very good."

"Yes, it's great!" Amy wanted to try all kinds of different things in Toronto, and this was certainly different; she'd never been to a place like this before.

When she looked at the menu, she practically started drooling.

"I thought we could share a platter," he said. "If you like."

There were five different platters that supposedly served two to three people, but they sounded like they could feed at least four. Each looked amazing, and she couldn't decide. Did she want schnitzel? Pork belly? But the platters with schnitzel didn't come with pork hock, and that sounded really good, too. She wanted to try spaetzle and cheese as well.

"You pick," she told Victor.

"No, you pick." When she gave him a look, he added, "You narrow it down to two, and I'll choose from those."

She finally managed that much, then started on the beer list, deciding on a German wheat beer that apparently had notes of banana and cloves. She'd never known beer could taste anything like banana.

Their beers each came in a half-liter glass stein. Victor had a Czech lager, which wasn't too bad, but not as good as her beer.

They talked as they waited for their platter, but conversation was difficult as it was loud, due to all the people and the music. She had to lean close to him, her leg brushing against his, and he put his hand on her thigh.

Certainly not the end of the world.

When their food arrived, she gasped.

"It's so big!"

Across from her, Victor chuckled.

"Do you need anything else?" the waitress asked.

Fortunately, Victor replied that they did not, as Amy was struggling to form words, overwhelmed by the shitload of food—and the fact that she'd shouted "It's so big!" loud enough for half the customers to hear, despite the noise.

The pork hock sat on a bed of sauerkraut. She'd never had sauerkraut before, but for now, she was more interested in the crispy skin on the pork hock and that giant pretzel. And the sausages. There were two different types; she couldn't remember what they were from the menu. There were also fries and a salad with gooseberries.

It would be impossible for them to eat all of this. She started cutting some pieces from the pork hock, depositing them on her plate along with mustard and sauerkraut. The pork hock was fatty and salty and wonderful, the skin as crispy as it looked. The sauerkraut wasn't bad, and it was growing on her with each bite. She had a sip of beer, then broke off a piece of the pretzel. It was still warm, and she groaned.

The gourmet burger place had disappointed her earlier in the week, but the beer hall wasn't disappointing, not at all.

"I take it you're enjoying yourself," Victor said as he cut a sausage in two and put half of it on her plate.

She nodded, her mouth around a fry.

He smiled. He looked happy just to see her happy, and it was suddenly hard to swallow.

She thought about her family and Shane. Her family loved her, but sometimes it felt like her happiness never occurred to them, like they cared more about what she could do for them, though perhaps that was unfair.

But Victor had planned something just for her.

"Thank you." She leaned forward and squeezed his leg.

"Oh my God," Amy moaned as they left the restaurant. "I'm so full."

They'd only eaten half the food. Victor was carrying the rest of it in a bag.

It would take half an hour to walk home, but she didn't mind. She needed some exercise after that meal, and it was a nice night. Not as warm as last weekend, when they'd been sitting on that rock, but nice all the same, although she needed her cardigan.

They spoke little on the walk, which was unusual for Amy, but she felt content just to be next to Victor and hold his hand. It seemed momentous enough, that single point of contact. Occasionally, she'd squeeze, and he'd always squeeze back.

It was so dependable, so reassuring.

By unspoken agreement, she climbed the steps to his house with him. He took off his shoes and brought the food to the kitchen, but then he was back in the hallway, his arms around her, his mouth on hers. She began unbuttoning his shirt and was annoyed when she discovered he was wearing a T-shirt underneath.

He laughed softly at her frustration.

"Come upstairs," he murmured.

When they got to his bedroom on the third floor, he slipped her cardigan from her shoulders and tossed it on the floor. Next, her necklaces, which he placed on his dresser. Then her shirt. Over her head and onto the floor.

He hissed out a breath when she stood partially clothed before him.

"You're so pretty," he breathed, his gaze intent on her body.

When she was with Victor, she never doubted that all his attention was on her.

Her bra was unclasped, as if in slow motion, and it, too, fell to the floor.

She needed his skin, though. She shoved his long-sleeved shirt off his shoulders, then lifted the hem of his T-shirt. His muscles flexed as he tugged it over his head. When she could finally touch her bare skin against his, she felt such relief. But the relief was short-lived; the touch inflamed her, and she reached for his belt at the same time as he reached for hers. Zippers were undone nearly in unison.

He groaned when he slipped his hand into her panties, his finger sliding through her moisture; she answered by groaning when she wrapped her hand around his thick cock.

"Later," he said gruffly, nudging her hand out of the way.

He dropped to his knees and pulled down her underwear and

jeans. When he pressed his mouth to her, she whimpered, threading her fingers through his short hair. She loved seeing him on his knees for her, this gloriously beautiful man.

It seemed like a miracle that he wanted her just as she wanted him.

He circled his tongue over her clit as his finger traced her entrance, almost featherlight. Incredible that such a light touch could do so much when it was from him.

Her legs felt shaky, and a moment later, he had one arm around the backs of her thighs, steadying her as he licked her.

Oh, God.

He pushed two fingers inside her as he picked up the pace with his tongue. She came apart, crying out for him, and just as she thought her legs might buckle, he picked her up and deposited her on the bed, removing the rest of her clothes from around her ankles.

He climbed onto the bed, holding himself above her. He was still wearing his jeans, but his cock bobbed in front of her, hard and ready.

She swallowed. "My purse. I have something in my purse."

He picked it up from the floor and brought it to her.

"Open it up," she said. "There's a black bag inside."

He did as instructed.

Amy had sewn the bag yesterday. She hadn't progressed very far with sewing, but it wasn't too difficult to sew a small bag that didn't have to look nice. She'd even put a drawstring on it.

"You can take it out," she said.

Was this foolish of her? She'd thought it would be fun, but what if…

He took out the pink vibrator and tossed the bag on the floor.

"This is what you use when you think of me?" he asked, turning it in his hands.

"Yeah."

"Show me," he said with a glimmer in his eyes. "Sit up and

show me how you use it." He stacked the pillows behind her so she could partially sit up and lean back.

"I don't know."

"I'll think it's hot, I promise." He lay on his side, head propped in his hand, and ran his other hand down her legs. Then he gave his cock a few pumps. And God, yes, she did like it when he touched himself, so maybe…

She picked up the wand-shaped vibrator. She knew that if she said no, he wouldn't push her. He'd happily use it on her himself.

But she wanted to do this.

She didn't turn on the vibrator, not yet. Instead, she dragged the end of it over her sensitive flesh. She didn't look at Victor, but she could feel his eyes on her, could hear the slight change in his breathing.

"That's pretty, baby," he murmured. "Now touch your pussy with your fingers."

She dipped one finger into her moisture, and when she removed her hand, he lifted it to his lips. He took her wet finger into his mouth and swirled his tongue around it.

"You taste so good," he said.

She turned on the vibrator at low speed and circled it around her clit.

"Just like that, yes. It's hot seeing you touch yourself."

He was doing all the talking, not her—quite a reversal from the first few times she'd seen him. And they'd slept together many times now, and he'd never spoken much in bed. But he seemed to understand that she needed to be talked through this, and the words fell easily from his lips.

"Do you touch your breasts when you get yourself off?" he asked.

"Sometimes."

"Do it."

He flicked his tongue over her nipple, then leaned back as she cupped her breast. Her nipples were tight peaks. She massaged her breast, her thumb brushing over the tip.

"Oh, yes, that's nice, baby, really nice."

He was stroking his cock, and the fact that he was still wearing jeans seemed rather obscene. She loved it.

"You see how hard you make me?" he said. "You enjoy what you do to me, don't you?"

She nodded jerkily, then increased the speed on the vibrator. When she gasped, she looked at him; his eyes were blazing with desire.

He moved above her, supporting himself on one hand, the other hand still on his cock.

"Now make yourself come," he said. "Can you do that for me?"

She nodded again.

"I'd like to come on you. Would that be okay?"

His eyes were piercing in their intensity, but there was always a kindness behind them.

"Yes," she said.

She continued to watch his hand move over his cock as she used the vibrator. She plucked her nipples and felt herself getting close. She could tell from his breathing—because she'd been with him so many times—that he was close, too, and that made her ascend even higher.

"So pretty," he said, his words labored now. "You're almost there, aren't you?"

Oh my God. Oh my God.

She arched her back and cried out, and he growled as he spent on her chest.

He collapsed beside her, and when she glanced over at him, she couldn't help an unhinged laugh, which he returned.

She'd never done anything like *that* before.

He got a wet cloth and cleaned her up, and she continued to feel giddy and slightly dazed.

"Victor, can I tell you something?"

"Yes?"

"You're awesome."

When Amy woke up the next morning, Victor was already awake. As soon as she opened her eyes, he reached for her and rolled on top of her.

She loved horny Victor first thing in the morning. It was a great start to the day.

This time, he was the one who used the vibrator on her before he slid inside.

But she was glad he'd wanted her to use it on her herself last night. She'd been a little shy, since it wasn't something she'd done with a partner before, but it had made her feel powerful.

Afterward, they stayed in bed together, the blankets twisted around their legs. She trailed her fingers up and down his tattoos.

"You sure did a lot of talking last night," she said. "Who would have thought?"

He chuckled as he pulled her closer.

Cuddling after sex on a Sunday morning? Life was good.

She ran her fingers over the three Chinese characters on his chest. "What does it say?"

He hesitated. "It's my brother's name. The first character is our last name, and then his given name."

Her hand stilled, and she was suddenly very, very cold.

Because she *knew*.

He had his brother's name tattooed above his heart. There could only be one explanation. She had no idea what she'd expected when she'd asked the question, but it wasn't this.

"His English name was Christian," Victor said. "He died five years ago."

EVERYONE else in Victor's life already knew because they'd been around when it had happened. He wasn't used to telling people.

But he'd known for a while that he'd tell Amy sooner or later.

"I'm sorry," she said, stroking his hair. "We don't have to talk about it."

"No, it's okay." It was better to do it now, since he'd started.

"You said you were the oldest—"

"He was second. Only a year and a half younger than me, and my sisters are quite a bit younger. They were born after my parents had lived in Edmonton for a few years; Christian and I were born in Hong Kong."

"You were close?"

"Yes. We were opposites in many ways, but we were very close. I'd been looking out for him for as long as I could remember."

He wrapped his arms around her, needing to touch her as much as he could. Hold on to something.

"He was an avid cyclist," Victor heard himself say. "He was always careful about safety, but the car in front of him…hit a pole. It fell on top of him."

He heard her sharp intake of breath, but he was faraway, imagining that terrible scene, as he'd done so many times before.

In a way, he felt detached as he spoke, but it was still difficult, and when he looked at Amy's face, her eyes shimmered with tears.

He wiped them away with his thumb.

"Don't worry about me," she said. "I'm fine. You can tell me whatever you want. Or nothing more, if you'd prefer."

He felt the need to keep going. "This was his house. He'd lived here for three years. When he died, I couldn't bear to sell it, so I sold my condo instead."

Did Amy think it was weird that he'd chosen to live here? She didn't say so.

"At first, I kept the house as it was," Victor said, "but eventually, I redecorated and refurnished it. Had some work done in the kitchen. It looks a lot different now than when he owned it." For some reason, it was important for her to know that.

She rested her head on his shoulder.

"I was different when he was alive. Not, like, a completely different person, but…"

"You didn't spend your evenings sitting on the patio, drinking scotch and staring at the grass you cut shirtless."

His laughter was brittle, but it was laughter nonetheless.

"It never goes away," he said.

"I know. How could it?"

"But I think I get along okay now."

It had become a part of him, and he could accept that, but he could see how certain parts of his life had been lacking…until Amy had burst into his life.

Christian would have liked her.

"Are any of your other tattoos for him?" she asked.

He touched a cactus below his brother's name. "He liked cacti. Most of my tattoos, even if they weren't directly for him, I got after he died. I'd had a couple beforehand, but after…"

It was another minute before he felt ready to continue.

"Tattoos were a deliberate form of pain." He'd started getting them several months after Christian had died. Not long after he'd thrown that bowl against the wall. "Something I could control, when I couldn't control what had happened to him. It felt good to have them done. If that makes sense."

"I can see it, yeah."

God, he felt like he was burdening her, but it was nice to tell her. Not like a weight was lifted from his chest, but she was important to him, and so it was important that she know this.

"I met your brother once," Amy said.

He immediately sat up. "When?"

"I told you that I didn't know Great Aunt Frances well, but I did take my grandmother to visit her. After I finished university, my grandma got sick, and I moved in so I could take care of her. She wanted to see her sister in Toronto, so I drove her down for the weekend a couple times, but these old houses with all the stairs are terrible for people with mobility issues. The last time, the man next door helped my grandma up the steps to the front door. I was thinking recently that he looked like you, but it definitely wasn't you. I'm quite sure it was your brother. He was very friendly. Smiled more than you do."

Victor swallowed. "Yeah, sounds like Christian." He got up and grabbed a framed photo from his dresser. "This was the guy?"

"Yes. He took a picture of us, actually. Me, Aunt Frances, and Grandma. It's still in the office at Aunt Frances's sex store."

"And your grandma?"

"She passed away. About five years ago, too."

He squeezed her shoulder. "I'm sorry."

And then she was wiping tears from his cheeks. It had been years since he'd cried.

He pictured that day in his mind. Amy, Frances, his brother.

He conjured up an image of a white-haired grandma. Three of the four of them were gone now.

But Amy was here.

And she'd met Christian, however briefly.

She'd given Victor a new memory of his brother; he hadn't thought there would ever be new memories, but here was one. Not his, but it was easy to imagine affable Christian helping her grandmother up those old porch steps.

"Thank you." He pressed the heel of his hand to his eye. "Sorry about this."

"Nothing to be sorry about."

Indeed, he didn't feel weak. Letting yourself be this way in front of someone was a difficult thing to do; he felt raw inside.

He needed to touch her, needed her to anchor him.

"Let's shower," he said.

They soaped each other up in the shower, and he asked if he could wash her hair—she'd brought her shampoo and conditioner over the other day—and she said yes. He massaged her scalp, ran his fingers through her wet hair.

He was *here*.

He was alive.

And he had this wonderful woman with him.

When they stepped out of the shower, he toweled her off and wrapped a fluffy blue robe around her because he thought it would look cute—and it did. He put on boxers and a T-shirt, and he led her to the sunroom on the second floor. The morning sun filtered through the glass. He squinted, overwhelmed by the brightness.

"This is the only room I haven't changed," he said.

"It's nice just like this. I wouldn't have changed it, either." She smiled at a flowering cactus. "I don't have a sunroom in my house. I have a second-floor balcony instead."

He did like this room, and when he wanted to sit outside,

instead of a balcony, he had the patio, which was now inter-twined with memories of Amy.

She stood on her toes and kissed him.

"I got you a present," Victor said once they were in the kitchen.

"You did?" Amy said. "What's the occasion?"

"You didn't like my boring mugs, so I got you a special mug to use when you're here."

As soon as he spoke, he wondered if this was too much. He'd bought her something specifically to use when she spent the night.

He pushed that thought aside as he pulled the mug down from the shelf.

"It's amazing!" She was so easily delighted. "I can't believe you went to the store to get me a unicorn mug."

"I didn't. I ordered it."

"Don't spoil my fun. I like thinking of you walking up to the cashier with this in hand." She traced her finger over the words on the mug. "'Never stop dreaming.' Just like it says on my pencil case."

The handle of the mug was the real showpiece, though: a unicorn with a rainbow mane.

Victor had searched online for unicorn mugs, and as soon as he'd seen a picture of this one, he'd had two thoughts.

First, that it was utterly ridiculous.

And second, that Amy would love it.

"Thank you." She threw her arms around him. "It's the best."

He smiled, then kissed her.

It seemed different from all the other kisses they'd shared before.

He kept touching her as they drank coffee and ate breakfast. He'd meant to make her something nice today, but he didn't have the energy after their conversation, so they were eating cereal and milk. Once again, she poured the milk in first.

"Try some of my coffee," she said, holding the unicorn mug toward him.

"Why? It's exactly the same as mine."

"But it tastes better from this mug."

He rolled his eyes and had a sip. "No, it doesn't."

Now it was her turn to roll her eyes and look at him like he was hopeless.

Oh, she was beautiful, and he had *fun* with her.

And when she smiled at him like that, it caused a strange starburst in his chest, and he couldn't say he was entirely fond of it.

Instead, he focused on the physical. On simply touching her. On those little moans she made when he slid his hand under the robe and up her leg, caressing her inner thigh. Her skin was so soft, and she arched into him. The way she responded to him, the way she gave herself over to his touch...

When she finished the coffee in her unicorn mug, he slid his hand up farther, almost to her core. He was overwhelmed with his need for her, and bending her over the counter and taking her here...that might give him some semblance of control.

Victor got up suddenly, his cereal not quite finished, and pulled her with him. He stood behind her and kissed the side of her neck as he reached for her panties. He could already feel her moisture through them.

Fuck, yes.

But they were getting in the way, so he grabbed the crotch and tore them off.

She yelped. "You better buy me new ones."

"I will." He shoved a finger inside her, and she gripped the counter.

He needed to be inside her. Now.

"You ready?" he asked.

"Yeah."

He grabbed a condom from the pocket of the robe—he'd stashed one there earlier—and rolled it on quickly. Then he flipped up the back of the robe, baring her ass. A thing of beauty.

He slammed into her pussy in one thrust, and she jolted forward, her hands scrabbling and finally grasping the opposite edge of the counter.

"Wanna fuck you hard," he said. "Can you take it?"

She nodded against the counter.

Yes. This was what he wanted. Fuck her hard, make her scream.

He dug his fingertips into her hips and continued to pump inside her.

Oh, God, yes. He needed this release. Needed her release.

He untied the belt on the robe and yanked it off so she was naked before him. She was so fucking hot. He watched his cock disappear inside her body, over and over.

He licked a finger and slipped it between her legs, circling her clit the way she liked it. She sobbed against the countertop, and as she started to shake, he slammed into her one final time and came, a moment of pure pleasure washing over him.

She slid to the tile floor, sitting on the pool of the blue robe, and reached for him. Clutched his shoulders.

Yeah, that had been good. Just what he needed. A physical release.

He slipped his hand through her hair, still slightly damp from the shower.

Just what he needed, yes. Amy.

He didn't quite feel like he'd regained the control he was losing. She was so lovely and perfect, and there was an unfamiliar feeling in his chest when he held her.

"Hey," she whispered, running a hand over his arm. "It's okay. I'm here with you."

He was scared by how badly he wanted to keep her.

He liked her very much.

But he didn't like things that overwhelmed him.

It reminded him of how he'd felt after Christian died. Even if this was completely different from grief, that was the last time he'd felt anything intense.

Amy was cracking apart the ordered life that had kept him safe from his strong emotions.

[19]

AMY HAD BEEN a bit nervous about seeing her new friends at Ossington Cider Bar. Last time they'd met up, Nicole had encouraged her to have no-strings-attached sex with her neighbor, and Amy hadn't exactly taken her advice.

But she shouldn't have worried about Nicole's reaction.

"Good for you," Nicole said, holding up her glass of cider. "As long as he's treating you right."

Amy felt herself blushing. "He's treating me *very* well."

Nicole snickered. "Outside of the bedroom, I mean."

"He took me to a cute coffee shop last night, then a German beer hall. It was so good, and he planned it all himself."

Nicole raised an eyebrow. "The bar for men is rather low."

"It is," Amy acknowledged. "I was starting to worry that things were a little one-sided, like with my ex. Then Victor did that, and I really appreciated it. He bought me a mug to use at his house, too, because I complained his mugs were too boring."

"She's never home at night," Sierra said.

"Occasionally!"

"Not last night, though. Or the night before."

This was true.

Amy still felt shattered after this morning. His brother—how awful. Whenever she thought about it, she wanted to sob. But she never wanted Victor to feel like he had to brush away *her* tears when talking about his brother.

It must have been difficult for him to tell her. Victor didn't share himself easily, so it must mean a lot that he'd done so.

He'd seemed distant later in the morning, but perhaps he was emotionally exhausted and wanted some time alone. They'd had leftovers for lunch—and still hadn't finished all the food from yesterday—and then she'd returned home.

Amy sipped her apple pie à la mode cider, which did taste a bit like apple pie with vanilla ice cream. There were definite notes of vanilla. Charlotte had declared it too sweet.

"Well, I'm glad he's not a douchebag," Charlotte said, "but if you ever need me to kick his ass…"

Amy was touched.

"You always say that," Rose said, "but I've never actually seen you kick anyone's ass. I think you're all talk."

"Just because you didn't see it doesn't mean it didn't happen."

"Right," Nicole said doubtfully.

"Victor is, uh, very well built," Amy said. "Just warning you."

"You still haven't brought any pictures to show me."

"Sorry."

She should get a picture of the two of them so she could admire him when they weren't together. Yep, that was a good idea.

"Amy, are you going back to Silver River for Thanksgiving?" Nicole asked.

"Gotta arrange a car rental, but I'm going. What about you?"

"Turkey dinner with my dad's side of the family."

"I visit my parents for the weekend," Charlotte said. "Kind of stressful, to be honest."

"We go out for Chinese food." Sierra shrugged. "Same as every holiday. You going to Ottawa, Rose?"

Rose nodded. "It'll be good to see my dad again."

Amy drank more cider and thought of her own family. She hadn't seen them in almost two months, and she did want to see them. She missed them.

Yet she was nervous, too.

Her life was in Toronto now, and she was going after everything she desired.

She had changed, but they would have expected her to stay the same.

"Your father forgot my birthday," Amy's mom said over the phone.

Amy lay back on her bed. "You've had the same birthday for all forty years you've been together."

"Yes, you'd think he would have figured it out by now."

"He could have put it in his calendar."

But Amy felt a twinge of guilt. She hadn't forgotten her mother's birthday—she'd called her mother at lunch on Friday and also sent her a card from Sierra's store—but she'd always been the one to remind her father.

And this year, she'd reminded him about his anniversary, but texting him about his wife's birthday had slipped her mind.

The thing was, her mom actually did a good job of reminding her husband. She liked a card and flowers; sometimes she had a specific gift in mind. She always made very obvious hints a week in advance, and then two or three days beforehand.

But Amy hadn't been there to hand-hold him.

She told herself it wasn't her fault that her dad had forgotten, but she'd had so many little responsibilities that had piled up over the years she'd lived near her family.

"You still liking it down there?" Mom asked.

"Yes! I love it."

"School is going okay? It wasn't weird going back after working for several years?"

"Well, it's different from undergrad. Took a little while to get back into the swing of it, but I'm feeling good about it now."

"I'm glad." Mom sounded a bit uncertain, though. She'd been baffled by Amy's life choices—the bustle and traffic of a big city was too much for her. "I'm looking forward to seeing you in a few weeks."

"Me, too."

Amy got off the phone and was about to do some work, but then she heard from another member of her family.

"Auntie Amy!" It was a video call from Abigail.

And oh, Amy wanted to give her niece a big hug.

"I lost my second tooth yesterday." Abigail opened her mouth. "See?"

"Did the Tooth Fairy bring you a toonie last night?"

"No." She looked cross. "For the Tooth Fairy to come, you can't just put your tooth under your pillow. Your mom or dad also has to call on a *special* phone line. And Daddy forgot to call, but he *promised* to do it tonight."

Amy tried not to laugh. "Did you ask him to call right in front of you? So you knew for sure he'd done it?"

"I asked. He said no. It's a special *secret* phone line, and it won't work if he does it when I'm in the room."

Oh, Fred.

"Auntie Amy!" It was one of the twins, but Amy couldn't tell which one because they were holding the phone too close to their face.

"No, don't do it like that!" shouted Abigail. "You have to hold it farther away."

"You do it for me!"

"Fine," Abigail huffed.

Mellie's face appeared on the screen. She was wearing the plastic heart jewelry that Amy had bought for her birthday.

"I like it better when you look after us," Mellie pouted. "Not Janey."

"I'm sure Janey does a good job."

"She doesn't know how to play Barnyard Animals."

This was a game Amy had invented for her nieces. "But you're so good at it. You can teach her."

"We tried. We tried very hard," Mellie said soberly.

"What happened?"

"Her rooster was all *wrong*."

"Cock-a-doodly-doodly-dooooo," Amy sang.

Mellie giggled. "She can't do it like that. Mommy said you're coming back for Thanksgiving. Are you?"

"I am."

It was hard to tell what was going on, but Mellie seemed to be jumping up and down. "When's Thanksgiving?"

"Soon."

"Tomorrow?"

"No. A few weeks."

"A few *weeks*? I'll be a grown-up by then."

"No, you'll still be four. It'll be way before your next birthday."

"My birthday is June twenty-third."

"Yes, it is," Amy said.

"Are you lying in bed? You have a pretty blanket."

"Thank you."

She talked to Mellie for a few more minutes, then had a brief conversation with Jessie, who didn't have as much interest in talking as her sisters. She preferred smashing her trucks together or building Duplo towers while wearing the little hardhat that Amy had gotten her.

Or maybe she had new interests by now? Kids could change so fast.

As she set her phone on her bedside table, Amy felt another twinge in her chest. She was used to seeing her family every week, and now it had been almost two months.

Living in Toronto did have its downsides.

Plus, Steven still wasn't speaking to her. She'd called him a few times, but he'd never picked up.

"Ivy is going to come with Sophia. Did she tell you?"

"She texted me yesterday," Victor said to his mom.

Ivy, who was three years older than Sophia, lived in BC.

"Your sisters are not as rich as you," Mom continued. "You should offer to pay for their plane tickets. They are coming to see *you*."

"Already done." Victor reclined in his chair as he pressed the phone to his ear.

"Make sure you pick them up at the airport. Their flights are arriving twenty minutes apart, so it should be easy."

"Yes, they've sent me their flight information."

He hadn't seen his mom since February, when he'd gone to Edmonton for Chinese New Year. That was the last time he'd seen his sisters, too.

All of his family except for one, the hole he would always feel.

His mother drove him nuts, but he suddenly wished she was coming with his sisters. If he told her that he missed her—and it would be hard to get those words out—she'd ask him what he'd been smoking or whether he'd rotted his brain with pineapple candies.

There were some things that just weren't done in his family, though Sophia was sometimes the exception.

"Have you called Lauren yet?" Mom asked.

"She contacted me. She's busy getting settled in Toronto right now."

Mom clucked her tongue. "She should meet you. You are a good catch."

Lauren had indeed emailed, telling him that she'd moved to

Toronto because she'd met a man online. She understood that her parents and Victor's parents were trying to force them together—and wasn't that annoying?—but she was already seeing someone. Victor had offered to meet up with her if she still wanted, just to hang out, since she knew few people here. It was frightfully social of him.

"Thanks, Mom," he said.

He didn't tell her about Amy. It was still pretty new, and his mom would go bonkers when she found out. He wasn't up to dealing with that right now.

"Maybe Ivy and Sophia will help you meet someone. They will get you out of that house. Make sure you go everywhere with them."

"But they'll want to go shopping together and things like that."

"Wah, but it's dangerous in the big city!"

"We've been through this before. It's really not dangerous here."

"Still, you never know. Would you want anything to happen to them? You should protect them. Nobody will dare try anything when you are there. You look like a badass with all those tattoos." She said this affectionately.

He laughed. "Thanks for calling me a badass." His mom hadn't approved of his tattoos at first, but she'd gotten used to them over the years.

"You sound stressed. Are you stressed?"

"No, I'm fine."

"I know just the thing. I will send it to you."

His mother hated that he lived on the other side of the country. It meant that she couldn't load him down with pomelos and barbecued pork and paper towel. In the past couple years, she'd started shipping him stuff from Amazon and other places.

"It's really not necessary," he said.

"I think it is. Make sure nobody steals it off your porch. You never know what your neighbor might do."

He refrained from making any comments about his new neighbor.

They talked for a few minutes, and then he headed upstairs to the sunroom.

"Hello, Mr. Spiky," he said to his favorite cactus.

He immediately looked back to make sure no one had been watching, even though he lived alone.

He was talking to a fucking cactus. That couldn't be a good sign.

Victor used to fancy himself a bit like this spiky cactus. A tough exterior, keeping people from getting too close. He didn't quite feel that way anymore, thanks to Amy.

Oh, Amy. He'd seen her only twenty-four hours ago, but he wanted to see her again.

He took out his phone and sent her a text while Mr. Spiky stared at him judgmentally.

[20]

"Dinner's not too big," Victor said as he slid a piece of baked salmon onto Amy's plate. "That's because I have special plans for dessert."

"Do you, now?" Amy said. "What are they?"

"I'm not telling."

Well, that was unacceptable. She wanted to know about these plans.

Once he put the pan down, she attempted to tickle his sides. No reaction. Then she tickled his stomach. Still no reaction.

"You're not ticklish at all," she complained. "How unfair."

She started to step away from him, but he captured her in his arms and planted a kiss on her lips. She smiled against his mouth before kissing him back. Then she sat down and surveyed the table.

Her plate had green salad and salmon. He'd also poured each of them a glass of white wine. It was simple, but it smelled delicious, and it was a home-cooked meal that she hadn't had to plan.

"Okay, I'll tell you," he said. "We're going to have Japanese soufflé pancakes."

She had no idea what those were, but they sounded exciting.

"Have you had them before?" she asked.

"No, but I thought it would be fun to try them. With you," he added, dropping his voice.

Oh, she loved his low, husky voice. It did things to her body.

But for now, she'd behave.

Dinner was quite good, and afterward, they headed out, hand in hand. The days were ever shorter now, so it was dark, and though many of the trees still sported green leaves, there were a few red and orange maple leaves on the sidewalks. They were farther south than Silver River; autumn would come later here.

The pancake place was called Fluffy Cloud, and she thought that was an awesome name.

The menu was just as awesome. It contained a brief description of soufflé pancakes: apparently egg whites were beaten into a meringue and folded into the batter. There were pictures of each item, which was helpful, but it also made her mouth water.

Though the man sitting across from her was contributing to that, too.

"I thought we'd split something," he said. "Whatever you like."

There were eight options, and each sounded amazing. The "basic" ones came with whipped cream and maple syrup. Even those looked incredible, but Amy was going to try something more exciting.

There were soufflé pancakes with caramelized banana and chocolate sauce.

A tiramisu option with mascarpone cream and espresso syrup, dusted with cocoa.

Another had lemon curd and raspberries.

Still another had blueberries and cream cheese.

"This is impossible," Amy said. "I want to try them all."

"Would you like me to decide?" Victor asked with a glimmer of amusement.

"Yes, please."

"Okay, we'll get the basic ones."

"Victor!"

He laughed. "I know you want something more interesting. How about the chocolate and caramelized banana pancakes?"

"Sure."

She wished she could take her nieces here. They'd love it, though they'd probably make an absolute mess.

Amy ordered their pancakes, and afterward, Victor entwined his fingers with hers.

"Two of my sisters are visiting next week," he said, "from Thursday to Sunday. Would you like to meet them?"

"Can I?"

"If you like. But if you think it's too soon—"

"No, I want to meet them."

He smiled at her. "I'm a bit terrified, but okay."

"Well, you're the one who offered." She paused. "Why are you terrified?"

"I can't begin to imagine the trouble and noise that the three of you will make together. I'm sure I'll get a headache."

He was still smiling though.

And she was smiling, too. She squeezed his hand.

How could she not be happy when she was with this wonderful man? She kept being amazed by all the little things he'd done for her. He'd bring her coffee in bed. Make her dinner. Find cool foods for her to try. Buy her a unicorn mug. He also totally respected that school was important to her and didn't demand attention when she had work to do. Simple things, but still.

She'd never felt so cherished before. Cared for. Understood.

So much for her plan to not date for a while after moving to Toronto, but she had no regrets.

Their food arrived, and it was just as amazing as she'd hoped. The pancakes really were a bit like fluffy clouds, though Victor said they looked like fluffy hockey pucks. Light and airy, but moist—she'd never had anything like them before. The bananas had been cooked in butter, and the chocolate sauce was decadent. Everything was dusted with powdered sugar. Too bad she'd forgotten to take a picture until she'd scarfed down most of her share.

Victor took her home via a back laneway. Not the sort of place she'd walk alone at night, but she felt safe with him.

"Why are we here?" she asked.

"I want to show you something. Ah, here we are."

Since night had fallen, she couldn't see them perfectly, but three garage doors in a row were painted with murals. Not quite as impressive as the ones at A Cup of Stars, but they were neat all the same. The first mural was an alligator—or was it a crocodile? Another was a group of raccoons playing hockey. The last was a background of green leaves with a series of ladybugs. That was probably why he'd brought her here.

She clapped her hands together. "These are great! I wish I was talented enough to paint something on my—Ahhhh!"

A raccoon popped out of a green bin and scurried away. A real raccoon, not a smiling one playing hockey.

Victor took her hand and led her away. "Don't worry, I'll protect you from all the wildlife in the city."

They ambled toward their houses.

"I'm going to Silver River to see my family for Thanksgiving," Amy said, once her heart had stopped pounding after their raccoon encounter. "I have to rent a car. I could take a bus to Sudbury and get someone to pick me up, but I'd much rather drive."

"You can take my car," Victor said.

"You have a car?" But of course he did. He was well-off. "I bet it's a really cool car." She pictured driving to Silver River in a black sports car. Fred and Steven would be impressed.

"Oh, yes. Very cool."

She skipped alongside him. "Can we look at it now?"

"Sure, if you like."

When they got to his house, they went around to the back, and he opened his garage door.

She burst into laughter. "You have a Honda Accord."

"What's wrong with that?"

"You said it was very cool."

He looked affronted—he was pretending, she knew. "This is cool."

"Nah, you're a practical middle-aged man."

"I'm not even forty. I've still got another five months."

"Fortunately," she murmured, sliding her arms around his neck. "I happen to like practical middle-aged men."

"Well, then. Perhaps you'd like to make out in the backseat of my car."

They did indeed make out in the backseat of his Honda Accord but decided they were too old to actually have sex there, especially since there was a perfectly good bed nearby.

When he turned out the lights in his bedroom, she snuggled up against his side, and he put his arm around her. She felt incredibly content.

She'd been in Toronto for almost two months, and it still felt like she was on vacation. Sure, she had school. A house to look after. But it was all such a breeze. She got to wander the city, popping into ramen restaurants and independent coffee shops. She drank apple pie à la mode cider and matcha lattes. She ate soufflé pancakes and soup dumplings. She had friends.

She had someone to cuddle her at night and first thing in the morning. Someone to bring her flowers. When she'd entered his bedroom last night, she'd found a vase of pink carnations, accompanied by a card, and her heart filled with joy.

She was almost scared of how wonderful it all was.

Aside from the raccoons.

∼

Amy had fallen asleep quickly, but it was after midnight now, and Victor was still awake. He occasionally had nights when he couldn't sleep, though he usually he slept well with Amy in his bed, and his insomnia was nowhere near as bad as it had been five years ago.

She hadn't invited him to come with her for Thanksgiving, and he couldn't help feeling a little disappointed.

Then he got mad at himself for being disappointed.

But he'd told her that she could meet his sisters, and she'd been excited. She'd meet his family, but he wouldn't meet hers.

It was stupid. He knew it was.

He and Amy had a great time together. Things were going well. And whenever he did something little for her, she was just so happy, and that made him want to do everything he could for her.

Still, he feared she didn't feel the same way about him. Yes, she was affectionate when they were together. Yes, she practically glowed.

But that was just Amy. She found joy effortlessly, even around a guy like him.

Could he make this work?

He eased himself out of bed, careful not to wake her, and padded down to the sunroom. He sat on the chair and looked out at the dark night.

As the oldest child, he was the one Christian was supposed to turn to for advice, and Christian had always looked up to him.

But right now, Victor was the one who needed answers.

He wished he could talk to his brother.

[21]

"Hey!"

Victor heard the shout over the sound of the lawn mower. He looked to the right and saw Amy on the other side of the fence, so he turned off the lawn mower and walked over to her.

"This is so not fair," she said.

"What's not fair?" he asked.

"You're cutting the grass in the middle of the day. When I'm not home."

"Well, you *are* home."

"But you didn't know I would be! Plus, you're wearing a shirt."

"That's why I figured you wouldn't care about me cutting the grass. You only want to watch when I'm shirtless."

"Why are you wearing a shirt?"

"Because it's not August anymore. It's not warm enough to cut the grass shirtless. Besides, I'll take off my shirt for you later." He winked at her.

"Except your sisters are coming soon."

Oh, right. Amy made his brain short-circuit sometimes.

His sisters were the reason he'd left work at noon, and he was cutting the grass before picking them up at Pearson.

"That's why I decided to come home for lunch," Amy said. "I brought you something." She lifted up a Tupperware of cookies and a cardboard box with "Harbord Coffee Bar" emblazoned on the top.

"You didn't need to do that." *You don't need to warm my heart like this.*

She shrugged, then leaned forward to give him a kiss. "Have fun with your sisters."

"I'll let you know about Saturday." He figured Saturday lunch might be a good time for Amy to come over and meet Ivy and Sophia.

She handed over the food before hopping up the steps to her back door.

Oh, man. He was such a goner.

"Victor!" Sophia shrieked. She ran toward him, her large rolling suitcase behind her.

Why did she have such a huge suitcase? She was only staying in Toronto for three nights.

She dropped the handle of her suitcase and launched herself at him. She'd always been a hugger, much to the bafflement of his parents.

Ivy walked over a few seconds later.

"Hey, Big Brother." She hugged him, too, but without nearly knocking him off his feet.

He drove his sisters to his house, and they talked the whole way.

Once inside, Ivy and Sophia headed to the guest rooms on the second floor. They'd been here a bunch of times, so they knew where everything was.

When they came down, he was making gunpowder tea and putting out the roll cakes.

"Ooh, fancy!" Sophia said. "What's the occasion?"

"Uh, you're here," he said.

"I know! Isn't it great? We're going to have so much fun. Remember last time, when we went to that cool bar and didn't get back until two thirty?"

"Unfortunately, yes."

"I'll get mugs for the tea," Ivy said.

He suddenly realized what was going to happen, but he was too late to stop it.

Shit.

"Look, Sophia," Ivy said. "Victor has a unicorn mug. Who would have guessed?"

"OMG! It's so cute. When do you use this, Victor? When you're trying to remind yourself to prance like a unicorn and follow your dreams?" Sophia snapped a picture of it with her phone.

He had to tell them the truth. He couldn't let them think he'd bought a rainbow unicorn mug for himself.

Besides, he'd planned to tell them about Amy eventually. He just hadn't planned to do it until tomorrow. He wasn't ready for this.

"I bought it for my girlfriend," he said. "To use when she's here."

It felt weird to say "girlfriend." It had been so long since he'd had one of those. But that's what Amy was, wasn't she?

"You have a girlfriend?" his sisters said in unison, Sophia's voice louder than Ivy's.

"Yeah."

"What's her name?" Sophia demanded.

"Amy."

"How did you meet?"

"She lives next door."

"Ah." Ivy nodded. "How convenient. So you didn't actually have to go to a bar or anything to meet her."

"What does she do?" Sophia asked.

"She's a student."

His sisters looked at each other.

"Are you dating a twenty-year-old?" Ivy asked. "That seems kinda wrong."

"No, Amy's in grad school, and she worked for several years first. She's thirty."

"That's acceptable."

"Glad you approve of my dating life."

"Approval from your little sisters is important," Sophia said. "They can make your life miserable otherwise."

"I'm well aware," Victor said dryly.

"What does Amy study?" Ivy asked.

"Structural engineering."

His sisters looked at each other again before sitting down at the table.

"Dad will like that," Sophia said. "Is she Chinese? Does she speak Cantonese?"

"No," he said, "she's white."

"That's not a problem. Mom will be fine with it."

"She's always been always okay with me dating someone of another race."

"Okay with it, yeah, but you know she had a preference. But now that you're forty-five and single—"

"I'm thirty-nine, thank you."

"—she's getting antsy. She'll be absolutely thrilled with anyone."

Just then, his phone rang. Victor pulled it out of his pocket. His mother, presumably checking that Ivy and Sophia arrived safely, so he answered.

"Hey, Mom."

"You have a girlfriend? And you didn't tell me?"

He'd known his sisters would blab to his mother, but he'd thought they'd wait until they were home. How foolish of him.

Instead, Mom had called him a mere five minutes after he'd told Ivy and Sophia.

He glared at his little sisters.

Sophia shrugged innocently. "I sent Mom a picture of the unicorn mug. Said it was your girlfriend's."

He scrubbed a hand over his face. His life was spinning out of control.

"I'm your mother," Mom said over the phone. "I should know these things right away."

"No," he said, "because then you would immediately fly down to meet her and scare the poor woman."

"I would not fly down immediately! Well…"

"Exactly."

"Is Lauren your girlfriend? I saw her mother yesterday, and she did not say anything, but maybe Lauren is a bad daughter who doesn't tell her mother important things, just like you."

He certainly wasn't going to spill the beans about the man Lauren had met online. Lauren could tell her mother in her own time.

"No, it's not Lauren," Victor said. "Her name is Amy."

Ivy and Sophia gleefully looked on as he answered lots of questions about Amy, most of which they'd asked him just a few minutes ago. Her age, her career. Stuff like that.

Sophia nudged Ivy. "I think he's having a good time, don't you?

Stay calm. Stay calm.

"When are you proposing to her?" Mom asked.

Okay, so much for staying calm. "We haven't been seeing each other for very long. Too early to think about that."

"Is she asking about marriage?" Ivy whispered. "Babies?"

He did not answer his sister.

"But you are getting old," his mother said. "No time to waste."

"I'm not rushing into anything."

Not if Amy doesn't want me to meet her family for the holidays.

Though perhaps she'd tell them about him. And really, it shouldn't bother him. He'd only just referred to her as his girlfriend for the first time.

"You said she is thirty, yes? That is good. Fertility declines with age. Better for her to be thirty than forty-five like you."

"Can you stop talking about her fertility? And why does everyone think I'm forty-five?"

Sophia was reaching for a cookie, but then she collapsed in a fit of laughter.

"Wah, I know how old you are, silly boy! I gave birth to you."

"First I'm forty-five, and now I'm a boy. Great."

"Sophia and Ivy will give me a full report on Amy. They are much more forthcoming than you."

He stifled a laugh. Yeah, his sisters might be forthcoming about his life, but they likely had secrets of their own.

He finally got off the phone and regarded his sisters. Sophia was twenty-four and currently working as a social media manager or something like that. It sounded like hell to him. Since the last time he'd seen her, she'd dyed her hair light brown. Ivy, twenty-seven, was a medical lab technician.

"Do we get to meet her now?" Sophia asked.

He couldn't help it. At the thought of Amy coming over, his heart started beating quickly, even though he'd seen her just a few hours ago.

"She's on campus, and since she came back at lunchtime—"

"Aww, did you have lunch together?" Sophia made smooching noises.

He ignored this. "I'll text her."

She didn't need to come today, but if she wanted to…

Amy arrived an hour later, when they were on their third pot of tea.

He met her at the door. She was wearing her blue polka dot dress with the buttons that were so fun to undo.

She hadn't even slipped off her shoes by the time Ivy and Sophia bounded over.

Victor had warned Amy that his sisters might be a bit much, but he wasn't too worried. He was sure she'd be able to handle it. Her temperament was more similar to Sophia's than his.

"Hi, Amy, I'm Sophia." She stuck out her hand. "Victor has told us so much about you."

"Oh, really?" Amy said.

"Yeah, we made him answer lots of questions."

"I'm Ivy." Ivy smiled. "I love your dress."

"It's great, isn't it? It even has pockets."

"Victor said you made the cookies," Sophia said. "They're really good."

"Thank you."

"I hope he does things for you, too."

"He made me dinner last week," Amy said. "Salad and salmon. Then he took me out for Japanese soufflé pancakes."

"What are those?' Ivy pulled out her phone. "I'll add them to my list. They sound good."

"Which list is this?" Victor asked.

"My list of foods to eat while we're in Toronto."

"Ooh, I have so many ideas of things you can add," Amy said. "Like, we had this really great pork hock at a German beer hall."

"That sounds delicious, but the list is already far too long." Sophia shook her head. "There's no way we can eat even half the stuff on that list."

"Well, I'm going to try," Ivy said.

Victor headed back to the kitchen, and everyone followed him. He poured Amy some tea.

"We have lots of practice with Victor's girlfriends," Sophia said to Amy.

Oh, geez.

"We're so much younger than him, and he's been dating since we were barely in school."

"Not to alarm you," Ivy said. "It's not like there have been tons of women."

"No, there really haven't. And it's been many years now, much to our mother's disappointment."

"Great disappointment."

"That's why I texted her as soon as I learned about you." Sophia smirked.

Even Amy looked a little tongue-tied in this situation, but she smiled brightly.

Eventually, however, they settled into a less embarrassing conversation about Silver River and Edmonton and Ivy's long list of food.

Victor didn't have much to contribute. In fact, it would have been a bit hard to get a word in edgewise. But he definitely liked seeing Amy getting along with his sisters. It felt good.

It felt right.

∼

Victor didn't see Amy on Friday—she had work to do—but at eleven thirty on Saturday, she arrived as Ivy and Sophia were getting ready.

"Ivy has decided we're having dim sum," Sophia said to Amy. "We're going to a place in Chinatown. Apparently you and Victor went there before?"

"It has carts, I understand," Ivy said. "I like the places with carts."

They headed to Spadina. Victor reached for Amy's hand and let his sisters walk a few paces in front of him.

"How was your day yesterday?" he asked quietly.

"It was good," Amy said. "Finished up an assignment, then went out with Sierra."

"I missed you."

"I'm sure your sisters are keeping you busy."

"They are." They were also irritating the heck out of him, though he did enjoy their visits.

But he'd been hoping that Amy would return the words he'd said to her.

She squeezed his hand. "I missed you, too."

And there it was.

He couldn't help smiling. "I started calling you my girlfriend. I hope that's okay but if—"

"It's more than okay, *boyfriend*." She knocked her hip against his.

They arrived at the restaurant and had to wait a few minutes for a table. They got a greater variety of food than last time—easier since there were four of them instead of two—and they'd just finished the egg tarts when Sophia said, "Amy, could you take a picture of the three of us?"

Victor handed his phone to Amy. She snapped a few pictures of him and his sisters, then Sophia took the phone and gestured to Victor and Amy. He put his arm around his girlfriend and smiled. When Sophia handed his phone back, he was surprised that he didn't look too bad in the picture.

He normally looked terrible in photos. He was bad at smiling genuinely on command.

But today? Somehow, it wasn't a problem.

Amy, of course, looked absolutely lovely.

He set the picture to the lock screen on his phone, then sent it to his mother, since she'd demanded a photo of Amy earlier.

What kind of future could Victor have with her? Would Amy want to live in her house or his? Or would she want to move somewhere else?

The thought of keeping her with him was terrifying and perfect at the same time.

~

That night, Victor couldn't sleep.

He headed down to the sunroom, sat on the chair, and picked up the book he'd been reading when he had trouble sleeping. It was about economics, and it had sounded rather interesting, but it was, in fact, a snoozefest.

"Hey, Victor," said a soft voice behind him.

He jumped and dropped the hardcover on his toe.

"Sorry I scared you," Ivy said.

Ivy had been terrified of the dark as a child, thanks to an unfortunate movie choice when she was four, and she'd often come to his room when she was supposed to be in bed. He'd let her sit on his lap while he studied. He'd read her sections of his textbooks to put her to sleep, and it always worked like a charm.

When he'd left home for university—he'd had no interest in living at home and going to U of A—she'd been so young. Sophia had been even younger, and she hadn't been bothered by the idea of him leaving; Ivy had held onto his leg and sobbed.

He looked down at the economics book, even drier than a textbook, and smiled faintly.

"Can't sleep?" she asked.

"No." He glanced at the clock. It was after two. Fortunately, Sophia hadn't wanted to party all night.

"I'm happy for you. About Amy. She seems really nice." Ivy sat down on the floor and folded her legs, wrapping her arms around them.

"You can have the chair," he said.

"No, I'm fine. I like sitting like this."

They sat in silence for a few minutes before she got up and looked at the cacti.

"We almost never talk about him," she said. "Though it's better than it used to be. I can bring him up around Mom and Dad without it ending the conversation."

"Yeah."

"He was the best at reading us stories. He'd do all sorts of different voices."

Yes, Victor was the one who'd put Ivy to sleep with his reading; Christian was the one who'd make them laugh.

"Amy knows about him?"

"She does."

Ivy walked over and gave him a gentle hug before going back to bed.

It was a while before Victor made it upstairs.

[22]

When Amy came downstairs the next morning, feeling refreshed after a good night's sleep, Victor, Ivy, and Sophia were clustered around the microwave.

"We should call Dad," Sophia said.

"No," Victor said. "I'm not calling Dad to tell him that I cannot figure out how to remove the child lock on my microwave. Besides, it's six in the morning in Edmonton." He tapped a few more buttons.

"Why are you bothering?" Ivy asked. "We've already tried everything."

Sophia pulled out her phone. "We should look it up. What kind of microwave is it?"

Victor raked a hand through his hair, which gave Amy a nice view of his arm muscles.

"Hey," he said when he saw her. "Good morning."

"What happened?" she asked.

"Sophia somehow managed to set the child lock on the microwave, and nothing we do makes a difference."

"Well, there's a simple solution to that." Amy went to the

microwave and unplugged it. When she plugged it back in, it worked. "We'll just have to reset the time."

Everyone looked at her.

"Wow, you're so smart," Sophia said.

"I can't believe I didn't think of that." Victor rewarded Amy with a peck on the lips, and her skin prickled.

Sophia made a face. "Ew, get a room."

"That was barely a kiss," Ivy said. "I think we can allow him that. In his own home."

"I should be off," Amy said. "I've got stuff to do. But it was so great to meet you two."

They each gave her a hug. Victor promised to text her once he was back from the airport, and then she was off.

She had dog-walking duty.

Paula was out of town for the weekend, and Debbie had sprained her ankle. She could let Beast out in the backyard to do her business, but Amy came by to take the dog on walks.

When she knocked on Paula and Debbie's door, she heard barking before the door opened, and she smiled.

"Thank you so much," Debbie said.

Beast *woofed* in agreement.

Amy took the dog for a walk around the neighborhood, then dropped Beast off, picked up her laptop, and headed to Harbord Coffee Bar.

"Hi, Lucy," she said. "I'll just have a coffee today. Better make it large."

"It's feeling more like autumn, isn't it?" Lucy said.

"Sure is."

No more summer dresses. Today, Amy was wearing jeans, a blouse, and a khaki trench coat with a colorful scarf that Victor had given her.

She did more than an hour of work before going to the store that Great Aunt Frances had owned. She wasn't planning on buying anything today, although she couldn't help wondering what Victor might enjoy using with her.

"Hi, Martha," she said. "I have a small favor to ask of you."

Five minutes later, Martha had scanned the picture of Amy, Grandma, and Aunt Frances and sent Amy a copy. She'd wanted to give Amy the original, but Amy felt like it belonged at the store.

On the way home, she stopped at Moonbeam Messages to see Sierra and get a card for Victor. For lunch, she had a beef and mushroom pie at a place nearby called Happy As Pie. A whole shop dedicated to pie—how cool was that?

Back at the house, she curled up with her e-reader, but before she opened it, she looked out the window at her street. She loved her little neighborhood. Her life in Toronto was just what she'd wanted it to be. In fact, it was even better.

Going back to her hometown next weekend—that would be like returning to the real world, even if it was the holidays.

~

"Drive safely," Victor said.

"I will." She sat in the driver's seat of his Honda Accord with the window rolled down, though it was chilly at seven thirty in the morning.

"Text me as soon as you get there."

"Will do. Don't worry, I'll take care of your cool car." She tapped the steering wheel.

He leaned down to give her a kiss. When he straightened, he looked like he was going to say something more, but then he simply held up his hand.

"Goodbye!" she called as she rolled up the window.

She put the car in reverse. Time to get out of the city.

Destination: Silver River.

Amy enjoyed the drive once she was out of Toronto. She hadn't driven in over two months, and it was nice to be behind the wheel again. She sang along with her music and listened to a couple podcasts.

But as she entered Silver River, her nerves started to rattle.

To get to her parents' house, she had to drive through the "business district" of the town. By the Tim Hortons, the grocery store, the diner. Though the diner had apparently changed hands? She did a double take. Yep, it had a different name now.

The garage door of her grandmother's old house, where Amy had lived for a couple years, had been painted red by the "new" owners—they weren't really that new. Amy preferred the original white.

The town had always seemed small, but never as small as it did now. Had she really lived here for so many years?

Three minutes after entering the town, she pulled up to the house where she'd spent her childhood. There were more leaves on the ground than in Toronto, and her dad was raking. Amy put on a toque before jumping out of the car.

Her dad's face split into a grin. "Amy! I've missed you."

"Me, too, Dad."

"Nobody to help me work on the car." Her father always had a car he was fixing up. "We should head inside. Your mother is making a special lunch for you."

Before opening the front door, she sent a quick text to Victor, and as soon as she stepped inside, she smelled something delicious. Her mom must be baking macaroni and cheese with the crispy topping, just the way she liked it.

"Hi, Mom!" she called out.

Her mother hurried into the front hall. "Darling, you're here! How was the drive?"

"Not too bad." She wrapped her arms around her mother, who held her for a long time.

There was nothing like her mother's hugs.

"I made you mac and cheese," Mom said. "Have you had it in Toronto? Or are you too fancy for it now?"

"I did have Kraft Dinner once, but that's not the same."

A few minutes later, her dad came in from the yard, and they had green salad and piping-hot mac and cheese. Dad put ketchup on his, and Mom teased him about it.

It was almost like Amy had never left.

After lunch, she headed to Fred's. When he opened the door, Abigail, Jessie, and Mellie barreled toward her and hugged her limbs.

"Did you bring us presents?" Mellie asked.

"Girls," Fred said. "Your aunt doesn't need to bring you presents every time she visits."

"But she's been gone for *years*."

"Well, I don't need presents," Abigail said. "I just need help with my career."

Still, she was quite interested in the stickers that Amy pulled out of her purse.

"What's your career?" Amy asked.

It took Abigail a moment to answer, as she was admiring the glittering under-the-sea stickers in her hand. "I want to be a director."

"A director! Like for movies?"

"Yes. Or plays."

"She just wants to boss people around," Fred said.

Abigail crossed her arms over her chest. "No, Daddy. You have it all *wrong*."

"Her other idea was Prime Minister, but she decided directing would be more fun."

"That's right," Abigail said. "But it's not fun right now because

Mellie and Jessie refuse to do what I tell them. They cannot take direction."

Amy stifled a laugh. "What about your parents?"

"They're always too busy doing grown-up things."

"I can help you this afternoon. I'm sure it'll be fun."

"Not *too* much fun," Abigail said. "You'll be working, remember."

"Yes. Of course."

"Mellie and Jessie will have small roles. I don't want them to feel left out."

"That's very kind of you."

Abigail beamed, then dragged Amy into the den, the twins on their heels.

"You'll perform this at Thanksgiving dinner tomorrow," Abigail said. "To begin, Mellie and Jessie will shout 'trick or treat' while holding their pumpkin buckets."

Amy was pretty sure she knew where this was going.

"Trick or treat!" the twins shouted.

"No, you're doing it wrong," Abigail said. "Louder."

"I think they're loud enough," Amy suggested gently.

Abigail glared at her. She seemed annoyed that Amy was trying to take over her role, but she relented, which was for the best. Amy didn't want her ears to hurt.

"Now, Auntie Amy, you say, 'Smell my feet, give me something good to eat.'"

Yep, it was just what Amy had expected.

They went through the rest of the words, and Abigail showed Amy the actions she wanted her to do, including sticking a foot up in the air for "smell my feet." For "not too big," she was supposed to hold her hands wide apart, followed by close together for "not too small." The last line, "just the size of Montreal," was supposed to be somewhere in between.

Next, they played Barnyard Animals. At first, Abigail declared she was too old for the game, but she happily played along.

Amy had to be the rooster every time.

After the last round of Barnyard Animals, when Amy's rooster started mooing for mysterious reasons, the girls collapsed into a fit of laughter.

Amy's heart swelled. Yes, she'd missed her nieces.

Fred walked into the den. "We're going out for a couple hours."

Amy stiffened and was about to protest. She'd planned to leave in forty-five minutes, and she didn't let people walk all over her anymore…like asking her to look after her nieces alone without any notice. That used to happen all the time when she lived here.

But she just said, "Okay."

It wasn't like she'd be back in Silver River very often.

Once her parents were out the door, Abigail decided they should have a girls' talk. Jessie put on her hardhat for this important discussion.

"Do you have a boyfriend in Toronto?" Abigail giggled.

"I do, actually." Amy smiled as she thought of Victor.

"Do you have a picture of him? Is he as handsome as a prince?"

Amy pulled out her phone. She had a text from Victor, telling her to have a good weekend. She brought up the picture of the two of them that his sister had taken.

"Oh," Abigail breathed. "He's very handsome."

"What does he have on his arms?" Jessie asked.

"Tattoos, dummy."

Amy placed a hand on Abigail's shoulder. "Don't call your sister names."

"Hmph." But then Abigail said, "Are they temporary tattoos? Like the one I have on my ankle?" She lifted her pant leg to reveal a tattoo of Belle from *Beauty and the Beast*.

"No, they're permanent tattoos. They don't come off."

"What's it like in Toronto? Are the buildings tall?" Abigail held her hand above her head.

"There are many tall buildings, yes," Amy said. "Maybe you can visit me one day."

They talked about Amy's life in Toronto for a few minutes, until Jessie and Mellie got bored and started banging on a toy drum.

"I direct you to stop that!" Abigail said.

The twins didn't listen, of course.

There was a big fight, which Amy managed to stop, though not before Jessie did some damage with her hardhat, and then they played another game of Barnyard Animals.

When Fred and his wife got home, Abigail ran up to him.

"Can I get a permanent tattoo, Daddy?"

"No, you may not. What has Aunt Amy been telling you?"

"She has a boyfriend, and he has lots of tattoos. They aren't princess tattoos, though."

Fred looked at Amy and raised an eyebrow.

"She also said we could visit her in Toronto. Daddy, I want to go to Toronto!"

"I don't know, sweetheart. It's a very long drive, and you don't do well with long drives."

"But I want to see the big buildings. And Auntie Amy."

A few minutes later, the girls were watching television as Amy got ready to head out.

"They really miss you," Fred said.

Amy nodded, and her chest squeezed with guilt. She was breaking these little girls' hearts so she could cavort around the big city, rather than seeing them multiple times a week.

"So do I," Fred added.

Oh. Just three words, but they were awful sappy, coming from her big brother.

She swallowed. "How's Steven? Is he still upset that Aunt Frances left the house to me?"

"I think he's starting to get over it, but yeah."

On the short walk across town, Amy thought of the many things that hadn't changed while she'd been gone.

The next morning, Amy prepared Thanksgiving dinner with her mother. They had a big turkey this year. It needed to go in the oven at a good time so they could have an early dinner. They made the same dressing as always, from an old Betty Crocker cookbook, with bread cubes, onion, celery, herbs, and lots of butter.

As Amy watched her mother chop the celery, she wondered if her mom's hair had been this gray in the summer. Had she just not noticed? Or had it become grayer in the intervening months?

Maybe because her daughter wasn't around.

"You've been making friends?" Mom asked.

"Yep!"

"Of course you have. And you mentioned having a housemate?"

"Her name is Sierra."

"Like the girl in those books you're always reading."

"She has the same last name, too. Isn't that a weird coincidence?" Amy turned on the stove and started melting the butter.

Mom laughed. "Abigail says you have a boyfriend."

"I do."

They chatted while they cooked, as they'd done so many times before. There was a comforting familiarity about it. Afterward, Amy went to the garage and helped her father with his latest carpentry project.

Yes, this was home.

"And as lead performer," Abigail said in a dramatic voice, "we have Amy Sharpe, all the way from Toronto."

Everyone clapped politely.

"The other roles will be performed by Mellie and Jessie Sharpe."

More applause.

Abigail had decreed that they would do their performance before Thanksgiving dinner. Fortunately, the performance was short.

"And…action!" Abigail said.

Mellie and Jessie stepped forward. "Trick or treat," they said, not quite synchronized. They were carrying pumpkin buckets, and Mellie wore a crown while Jessie wore a hardhat.

Now it was Amy's turn. She rolled up her sleeves to display the temporary tattoos that Abigail had given her. Supposedly these were part of her costume.

"Smell my feet," she said.

Everyone chuckled, except Steven.

Amy couldn't help wondering what Victor would think of this. What if *he* had to perform? The thought nearly made her chuckle, but Abigail wouldn't appreciate that, so she kept a straight face.

After the performance, they said grace, then began passing around the platters of food. Turkey, dressing, squash, green beans, mashed potatoes, rolls, gravy, and cranberry sauce.

"Could you pass the green beans?" Steven asked Amy.

"Sure!" She was pleased he was finally talking to her, even if just to ask for a dish. He and his wife had been over for two hours before dinner, watching football while Amy and Mom prepared all the vegetables, and he hadn't said a word to her.

"How's Toronto?"

Ooh! Actual conversation!

"It's great."

"Are you almost finished playing tourist? Will you be home before Christmas?"

She tensed. "I'm in school. I intend to finish my degree."

"Away from your family," Steven said. "This is where you belong. We stayed, but you didn't. Mom and Dad are getting old. And I still can't believe Great Aunt Frances left you that house because you looked after Grandma. Is that why you took care of her? Did you know?"

"Your grandmother asked her sister to leave Amy the house," Dad said, "but I'm positive Amy didn't know that. And Frances probably knew Amy the best of you three. She still left you a little money—she didn't have to."

"That house is worth a fortune," Steven grumbled. "Even if it's old and narrow and has such a small yard. You should sell it, Amy, and split the money between us. That's only fair. You'd still be able to buy a house in Silver River with your third."

"I'm happy where I am," Amy said, dumping some mashed potatoes onto her plate. "And no, I did not know I'd be getting the house. I took care of Grandma because I wanted to. Because I loved her, and…" She felt tears coming to her eyes.

"When are you coming back again?" Mellie asked.

"Probably at Christmas, sweetie," Amy said.

"You'll miss tobogganing in the first snowfall with the girls," Fred said.

Yes, that would be fun, but she'd be here for Christmas. The university would be closed for two weeks. She could spend a decent amount of time in Silver River, though she wanted to spend some time in Toronto, too.

"Who will help me with the Christmas lights?" Dad asked.

All the things Amy would usually do with her family…they wouldn't be happening this year. Time with her family would only come in small parcels now.

Fred had stayed. Steven had moved forty minutes away—that was basically the same. Her family had lived here for a long time.

She knew she didn't owe them each a third of her inheritance, and her brothers weren't in financial hardship and desperately in need of cash—if so, she would have helped them out.

And she didn't owe it to them to stay in Silver River, yet she kept feeling like she did. It wasn't as if she'd needed to leave to get a job, and she didn't like upsetting the balance in her family.

They shouldn't be unhappy because you've made a life for yourself in Toronto.

Victor would reassure her if he were here.

But she hadn't invited him because she hadn't been ready to handle it. She hadn't known what it would be like to return to Silver River for the first time since the move, and adding a new boyfriend on top of that?

She had a bite of dressing with a generous amount of gravy and cranberry sauce. Her favorite. But it tasted like ash in her mouth.

"You look sick, Auntie Amy," Jessie said. "You know what will make you better? If you put on your hardhat. My hardhat always makes me tough and strong."

Oh, God, that nearly made her cry. Her darling niece.

How could she be so cruel and stay away from her family when they loved her?

Just then, the doorbell rang.

"I'll get it," Amy said, wanting an excuse to leave the dinner table. She hurried to the door and flung it open.

"Hi, Amy."

She hadn't known what she'd expected, but it wasn't him.

Shane.

[23]

It was a bit chilly after dinner, but Victor figured he'd be warm enough outside with a cup of coffee.

When the coffee was ready, he opened his cupboard. All his mugs were identical.

Except one.

And that was the one he found himself reaching for. The rainbow unicorn mug he'd bought for Amy.

Yep, he was so far gone that he was actually going to drink his coffee from a mug that said "Never stop dreaming."

A laugh escaped as he realized the truth.

He loved Amy.

He was drinking out of her damn unicorn mug because he missed her so much.

Victor sat on his patio, not bothering to look over the fence because there was no point when Amy wasn't here. He pulled his phone out of pocket, ready to text her, but then he stopped himself.

She'd been gone since seven thirty yesterday morning, and she'd only sent him one text, to let him know she'd arrived safely.

He hadn't heard anything else, though he'd sent her a couple messages this afternoon.

He put down the mug and scrubbed his hands over his face.

She wasn't replying to him, and she hadn't invited him for Thanksgiving. But they did spend quite a bit of time together. On Friday night, she'd given him a card of two cartoon otters cuddling in bed.

Surely she didn't give snuggling otter cards to everyone in her life.

And she was happy to call him her boyfriend.

But how, exactly, did she feel about him?

Victor pressed the palms of his hands to his cheeks. He was in love with her. In fact, he was overwhelmed by his love for her.

He hadn't had feelings this strong since the year after Christian died, and those feelings had scared the shit out of him. Led to him not sleeping for days and walking around like an angry zombie.

Obviously, this wasn't the same. Love was a positive feeling.

But still.

She was lovely and amazing, and he missed her more than he ought to, considering she'd been gone only thirty-six hours and would be home tomorrow.

He shifted in his chair, but there was nothing he could do to make himself comfortable. He didn't enjoy feeling like he wasn't the master of himself, like he'd felt after Christian's death.

Why did he care so much that she hadn't invited him for Thanksgiving? They hadn't been together for long.

That was part of what scared him: he felt so much in so little time.

He'd known her for less than three months, and for the first couple weeks, he'd done little but nod at her, having no idea how she'd soon upend his life, getting him to buy flowers and a unicorn mug, and actually go out more than once in a blue moon.

Yes, she'd turned his life upside down, and he'd liked his quiet little existence. Going to the office, working out, watering his cacti.

And now his life had been blasted full of rainbows and sparkles and ladybugs.

He took a deep breath.

No, he didn't want to break up with her—in fact, the thought caused him a disturbing amount of pain—but perhaps he should slow things down.

Until he felt like he was in control again.

"Shane." Amy swallowed. "What are you doing here?"

"It's your family's Thanksgiving dinner tonight, isn't it? Steven said you'd be around."

She noticed the flowers in Shane's hands. He'd never brought her flowers before. These were lilies, and she didn't much care for lilies. Not that she'd ever told him this, but she'd told him— more than once—exactly what she liked.

He was going to ask to get back together. There was no other explanation.

Steven was likely pleased, thinking it would get her to sell the house and move back to the Sudbury area.

She was suddenly just so tired, so exhausted from all the guilt she'd felt throughout dinner. The turkey and dressing were a lump in her stomach.

But she could stand up for herself. She felt no guilt when it came to Shane.

"Get out," she said.

"Amy, I—"

"No, I don't care. Get the fuck away from me. I have a boyfriend, and he treats me better than you ever did. I never should have stayed with you for so long."

Shane looked perplexed. He really didn't get it, did he?

Well, he didn't deserve any more of her time.

She slammed the door in his face.

When she turned around, her parents and her brothers were there, staring at her.

"Perhaps you should have let him say his piece," Dad said.

"I agree," Steven said.

Oh, for fuck's sake.

She was angry, and she felt more confident after telling off Shane.

"I'm happy in Toronto, dammit," Amy said. "You don't want me to be happy? You want me to move back and reunite with my ex? I don't owe you free childcare, Fred, especially when you don't give me any warning. And Dad, it's not my fault you forgot Mom's birthday. Why can't you write it in your calendar? I don't owe it to you all to be here and do everything you ask. Steven, when Uncle Gary died, he left money for you and nothing for me, and you didn't split your inheritance with me, did you? Why is it different now?"

"But—" Steven began.

"No. Stop it."

Amy's eyes widened. She'd never heard her mother speak this loudly before.

"I spent all morning and afternoon with Amy, preparing dinner," Mom said. "She's happier, and I'm ashamed I never realized she wasn't happy here." She turned to Dad. "You know your mother asked Frances to leave Amy that house because she wanted Amy to move to Toronto one day. She would have left her own house to Amy, but she was afraid that would make Amy stay in Silver River, when she longed to leave."

Amy's heart squeezed as she thought of her grandmother.

"You know how much Amy did for everyone while she was here?" Mom continued. "She deserves that freaking house. And Steven, you've been in contact with Shane, who would have wanted her to stay in a place she hated and expected her to do all the housework and all the parenting if they had kids. I don't want my daughter..." Her strong voice finally faltered. "I don't want my daughter to have the same life I did."

Oh, Mom.

"I'm not cooking Christmas dinner this year." Mom shook her head. "I refuse. Amy and I will play with the grandkids while you guys figure it out. It better be fucking great. Next Thanksgiving, I'm not cooking, either. I'm parking my ass in front of the television to watch football."

"You don't even like football," Amy said.

"Fine. We'll watch Tom Hanks films. And someone else better do the dishes tonight."

"We have a dishwasher," Dad pointed out.

"You can't put the nice dishes in the dishwasher. Haven't you paid attention all these years? No, you can deal with clean-up. Amy and I will get the first servings of all the desserts, and then we'll go to the bar."

"I don't think the bar's open this weekend," Amy said.

"Then we'll go up to your old bedroom and drink. I know you're feeling guilty right now, but don't you dare feel guilty about anything."

For the next minute, it was silent. Everybody was too stunned to speak.

Then Jessie ran up in her hardhat. "Granny, you swore! Does that mean I can swear?"

Amy sat cross-legged on her old twin bed, large servings of cherry cheesecake and pumpkin pie with whipped cream on her plate, a glass of white wine on her bedside table. Mom sat on the edge of the bed with her own plate of dessert.

It seemed delightfully wrong. Hiding away upstairs, just the two of them.

Mom giggled, actually giggled, and stuffed an enormous bite of pie into her mouth, chasing it with wine.

Amy felt tipsy, even though she hadn't had much to drink.

"You know what I found in the basement?" she said. "Furry pink handcuffs."

"No!" Mom laughed. "Really?"

"An entire box. Apparently Aunt Frances owned an adult fun store, if you know what I mean."

It was a weird thing to tell her mom, but right now, they felt more like sisters.

Mom doubled over and laughed even harder.

"Why don't you visit me in Toronto for a few days?" Amy suggested. "Maybe even a whole week. I'll have school on weekdays, but it'll be fun, won't it? You can go shopping, eat sushi—"

"What will you father eat? I suppose I could freeze a lasagna and some portion-sized meals."

"Mom, he's a grown man. Sure, make him one or two meals if you like, but he can figure out how to look after himself."

"You're right."

Amy gulped her wine. "Do you regret staying in Silver River? Do you wonder how your life might have turned out if you'd left?"

"I don't regret staying, but I regret that I didn't push against gender roles. There was so much I never expected your father to do. So much work I just accepted, and it never got acknowledged. I do miss you, Amy, but I'm glad you have what you want. If you weren't getting it here, you shouldn't have stayed. I never noticed how much you did, just like nobody noticed how much I did." Mom shook her head. "Women my age, when they get divorced, they don't want another partner."

Amy stilled. "Are you thinking of divorcing Dad?"

"No, no, I'm just saying. Maybe it would be good for me to go to Toronto for a week, for him to manage alone. In the spring, I think. When it's warm."

"Sounds good." Amy refilled their wineglasses.

"Show me a picture of this man of yours. Abigail is very impressed he has *permanent* tattoos."

Amy scraped the last of the cherry cheesecake off her plate before pulling out her phone and showing Mom the photo of her and Victor. She was glad they were having this talk. Of course, she wouldn't tell her mother that she was sleeping with Victor and at first had only intended to have casual sex...but this was nice.

Mom raised her eyebrows, probably surprised Victor wasn't white, but she didn't comment on that. "Such a lovely couple. You should bring him here for Christmas."

"I hope to."

"But make sure you don't get in the habit of doing everything for him."

"Don't worry, he's lived alone his entire adult life, so he's used to doing everything himself, and he's thirty-nine now."

"So much older than you. Scandalous!" Mom giggled.

"Not even a decade older, Mom. Really. He's good at caring for himself, unlike Shane."

"I never saw how bad Shane was for you until recently."

The memory of Amy's last relationship made her tense.

"With Victor," she said, "I feel like we're taking care of each other. He buys me flowers and plans nice dates..."

Most of it wasn't that simple to explain, though, but he made her feel like she was important.

"You know," Mom said, "there's an extra pumpkin pie in the garage. Want me to get it? We'll eat it right out of the pie pan."

Amy laughed and put her arm around her mother. "Alright, let's do it."

~

Amy said goodbye to her mom and dad, then made a brief stop at Fred's to give a book to each of the girls—you could never have too many books, right? Jessie said she wanted to be an engineer when she grew up. "Just like you, Auntie Amy."

Once the girls were looking at their books, Fred pulled Amy aside.

"I'm sorry," he said. "For taking you for granted. For not acknowledging that you had your own life. I hope everything in Toronto works out for you."

"Thank you." She gave her brother a hug.

Steven hadn't apologized, but hopefully, one day he would.

Before heading back to Toronto, Amy parked at the school and walked to the large outcrop of the Canadian Shield at the edge of the field. The rock in Yorkville had reminded her of this.

Now, this reminded her of the rock in Yorkville. Of Victor.

Although she retained some affection for her hometown, she was ready to leave. It was a nice place to visit, but it wasn't home anymore. The thought of staying made her itch.

No, home was in the city, and she was lucky to have the opportunities she'd been given. She recalled being a little girl, sitting on this rock and dreaming of a world beyond this town.

Grandma, I did it. I have the life I want. The life you wanted for me.

She shed a few tears for her grandmother, whom she sadly couldn't see any more when she returned to Silver River, then stood up.

It was time to go back to her house. To her boyfriend.

$$[\ 24\ ]$$

VICTOR FELT JITTERY. He wished he could blame it on the three cups of coffee he'd drunk in the past hour, but he knew that wasn't the reason.

It was Amy.

She'd texted him more than four hours ago to say she was leaving. For the last half hour, he'd kept checking the traffic coming into Toronto. It wasn't too bad, surprisingly.

So, she should be back any minute.

When his doorbell rang, he shot out of his chair. He opened the door, and there she was, wearing a trench coat and the scarf he'd bought her. She looked radiant, her grin wide. And she was *his*.

His possessiveness frightened him.

The flame in his heart? It frightened him, too.

"I missed you," she said, throwing her arms around him. Her suitcase was beside her; she hadn't gone to her house first, even though it was right next door.

He pulled her inside and ran his hands all over her. Savored the feeling of touching her once again.

Words came to his lips, but he shoved them back. He wouldn't say those things. No, he'd just get inside her as fast as possible. He needed her. He craved her.

Victor didn't like craving someone like this, but he couldn't help it.

He'd lose himself in her body until he couldn't think straight, until he didn't have all these goddamn *feelings* in his heart.

His mouth crashed down on hers, and he pushed his tongue between her lips. She squeaked in surprise before kissing him back with just as much urgency.

Yes.

He slid his hand between her legs, touching her roughly through her jeans as his other hand squeezed her ass.

"Victor," she murmured.

There were too many clothes. Far too many clothes. He tore off her jacket and pulled her sweater over her head. Her bra hit the floor next, displaying her heavy breasts. He sucked one peak into his mouth, and she gasped and gripped his hair, causing a prickle of pain.

He relished the pain. Better than the other shit he could be feeling.

He shoved his hand inside her jeans, finding her warm and wet and so necessary, but then she was sliding away from him, down, down, down.

To her knees.

She unbuttoned his pants and pushed them down along with his boxers. His erection sprang free, and she licked her lips.

She fucking licked her lips.

When her mouth was on him, he practically lost his mind.

God, yes.

He shifted a hand to the back of her head and controlled her movements.

When he could stand it no more, he pulled her up, removed her jeans and underwear, and grabbed a condom from his pocket.

"Here?" she asked.

"I can't wait any longer."

He turned her away from him, rolled on the condom, and shoved inside her in one thrust. She gasped again, her forehead hitting the door.

"You okay?" he asked.

"Yeah, just keep going."

And so he did. He pounded into her, over and over, and when he needed to touch her breasts, he wrapped an arm around her chest and squeezed them in his hand.

She felt so good. How was he such a lucky bastard?

He wanted…

He shoved that aside by pounding into her even harder, and when her breaths quickened, he slid one hand down to touch her clit. She came immediately, and he followed soon after, crying out her name as his orgasm consumed him.

Amy.

Amy, Amy, Amy.

There was a sickening twist in his chest as they collapsed together on the floor, his arms around her because he needed —*needed*—to hold her close after what they'd done.

But what he really needed was to get a hold of himself.

Victor had been insatiable, and Amy wasn't complaining, but now that they were lying in bed together, he felt like the man she'd first met. Guarded, unable to let her in.

"You hungry?" He ran his hand over her cheek, then withdrew.

"Yeah, some food would be good."

For dinner, he made poached eggs, something Shane never would have done, and she told him about her weekend in Silver River.

He listened, and he bristled slightly at the mention of her ex.

Still, something seemed off. Like he wasn't giving his full attention to her, the way he usually did.

After dinner, she went to her house to unpack and do a load of laundry. She caught up with Sierra before going back to Victor's.

When he was inside her, everything was good. He felt amazing and *right*.

But after…

Once again, something seemed off.

"Is anything wrong?" she asked.

"No, I'm fine."

"You're just a little…" She made a gesture with her hands.

He laughed quietly. She realized she hadn't heard him laugh earlier today.

"I'm fine."

She didn't believe him, but what would be the point in pushing?

For the next few days, things were normal, more or less. She went to school. She had a latte and dark chocolate raspberry roll cake at Harbord Coffee Bar. She read by the window in her second-floor reading room. She called her mother. She called Fred and made arrangements to have regular Sunday-morning Skype dates with the girls.

It should have been great. She no longer felt guilty about not being near her family.

But her relationship with Victor wasn't quite right.

He hadn't bought her flowers or taken her out for soufflé pancakes or shown her a garage door he thought she'd like. Not that he needed to do those things all the time.

And yet.

On Friday, the class she was TA-ing had their midterm, which she was responsible for marking. She didn't mark the physical copies of their exams; instead, the papers were scanned in, and she got to mark them electronically. It took an hour to figure out the software.

So fancy! When she'd been in undergrad, things hadn't been done like this.

She'd never marked a midterm before. It was a decent percentage of the students' final grades, so it was important, and she wanted to do a good job.

She texted Victor to tell him she wouldn't be able to spend as much time with him this weekend, and he said that was fine, he understood, she should take all the time she needed.

He was always so understanding.

She didn't see him on Friday. Saturday after dinner, she went to his house, and he took her to bed.

Afterward, they lay next to each other, and she absently stroked his arm.

"Let's go somewhere tomorrow to see the fall colors," she said. "Just in the city. Maybe High Park? I hear Sherwood Park is nice. We could take your very cool Honda Accord."

That didn't elicit even a twitch of his lips.

"No, I have work to do, and so do you," he said, though she'd told him that she'd made good progress on the midterms.

"Okay, I'll go by myself."

She hoped that would change his mind, but it didn't.

She felt foolish. It shouldn't bother her that he wouldn't see the autumn leaves with her. They didn't need to do everything together.

Still. She knew Victor. Something was wrong.

Or was she being paranoid?

Maybe it was just as Sierra had said. The beginning of a relationship was the best, and now they were past that. It had been silly to think things could have stayed that way forever.

Though that didn't sit right with her.

So Amy went to High Park alone and snapped pictures of the

large golden and orange maples near the entrance of the park. She took a path through the woods, happy to go wherever it would lead her, and ate schnitzel at a Polish restaurant on Roncesvalles.

She decided to walk back to the Annex, even though it was a long way, but it was a crisp, sunny autumn afternoon. She passed Tibetan restaurants on Queen Street. Stores selling only stickers or cocktail supplies or ornate paper and washi tape. After coming across two liquid nitrogen ice cream shops, she decided to go in. The ice cream was supposed to be super creamy because there wasn't enough time for big ice crystals to form. She had a scoop of chocolate fudge. It was delicious, but she wasn't sure the liquid nitrogen made much difference.

She took a picture of it and sent it to Victor.

No response, but that was okay! She was having a fun time by herself.

She detoured off Queen near Spadina to see Graffiti Alley, where she took more pictures, before heading through China-town and up to her house. And Victor's.

She rang his doorbell. No answer.

Dammit, she'd been looking forward to telling him about her day, but instead, she went home and marked midterms. She'd be able to finish them before dinner.

Victor stared at the picture of liquid nitrogen ice cream. He'd looked at it eleven times since Amy had sent it to him.

Yes, he'd counted.

God, he loved her.

And so, when the doorbell had rung—almost certainly her—he hadn't answered.

No matter how many walls he put up around himself, he still felt too much when he was with her. Why couldn't he make these feelings stop?

His mom's "care package" had finally arrived—she'd used the cheapest shipping option, so it had taken a while. Apparently, she thought rose-scented bubble bath would make him less stressed.

He couldn't imagine using it without Amy.

But he was not having a fucking bubble bath with her, no matter how much he wanted to.

He ran his hands through his hair, then drained the rest of his coffee from his plain blue mug. Which also made him think of Amy, who'd remarked on his boring mugs.

Yep, everything made him think of her. One memory or another, even though he'd known her less than three months.

What should he do? Should he break up with her?

Surely there was a way to be with Amy without being consumed by her.

He just had to find it.

~

The following Saturday, things still hadn't changed.

Amy kept wondering if she was imagining it, but she didn't think she was.

She wouldn't bottle up her feelings and pretend everything was okay. She'd done that in relationships before, but she wouldn't do it with Victor.

So Saturday morning, after spending the night with him, she took a sip of coffee from the mug he'd bought for her and said, "Victor, what's happening with us?"

~

"What do you mean?" Victor asked, regarding Amy from across the breakfast bar.

"Ever since I got back from Thanksgiving, things have seemed...different."

I realized I loved you.

"Why didn't you invite me for Thanksgiving?" He hadn't mean to say that, but he couldn't seem to help himself.

"Is that what this is about?"

"You met my sisters, but you didn't invite me to meet your family."

He hated sounding petty.

"You should have told me you felt that way," she said. "I could have explained. It was the first time I was going back to my hometown after moving to Toronto, and I felt guilty about being away for so long. Introducing you to my family just seemed like one more complication. I wanted to go there by myself, but I intended to invite you over for part of the Christmas holidays. You'll come sometime in December? They know about you."

Something released inside his chest. He felt like an ass.

It was all perfectly reasonable, and it wasn't like she was keeping him a secret. She imagined them being together at Christmas. That was something.

No, no. This was too much.

"We just need to talk about things. It's not a big deal." She smiled at him.

He couldn't manage to smile back.

"Is that the only reason you've been pulling back?" she asked. When he said nothing, she continued, "Are you going to deny that's what you've been doing?"

No, he wouldn't.

He'd let her become close to him, and now, he had to protect himself. Like he had six months after his brother died by making himself numb. He'd numbed himself against the strong emotions that had made him throw a dish against a wall, then cry over the broken pieces.

He could barely believe that had been him.

"I don't want a one-sided relationship again," she said quietly, her eyes pleading. "I deserve better."

"You do, but I can't give that to you. I'm not the man you want me to be."

Her bottom lipped quivered. He wanted to reach out and touch her, make it all better.

But now he understood. This was the way it had to be.

He hadn't been numbing his feelings anymore, not consciously, but he'd built a comfortable, contained life that helped him survive. And then he'd let down his guard. Lost his control. She was wreaking havoc on the carefully-constructed world that had kept him safe.

If only the fence between their yards had been higher.

Amy took the unicorn mug, dumped the coffee into the sink, and rinsed it out. "Well, then. I won't fight to be with someone who doesn't want to be with me."

I do want to be with you. But I can't.

She looked crestfallen. Her lip was quivering again.

"You're scared," she said.

He didn't deny it. Just shrugged, as though this was all no big deal. He hoped his hand didn't shake as he lifted his boring mug to his mouth.

She nodded.

And then she walked out the door.

It was better to lose her now than later. He knew what it was like to lose someone whom you loved, who was an integral part of your life.

It had destroyed him.

Sure, he felt fucking awful now, but this would work itself out. He hadn't known her for long.

In a couple days, he'd be back to his usual self. He was sure of it.

[25]

"THAT FUCKER," Charlotte said. "Men suck."

Amy guzzled more of her passionfruit peach cider. It was sweeter than anything else she'd had at Ossington Cider Bar. Basically alcoholic juice. Charlotte didn't comment on her beverage, however.

"Yeah, that fucker," Rose said.

That made Amy laugh for the first time all day. Coming from Charlotte, it wasn't a surprise, but those words seemed out of character for Rose.

"What do you want us to do?" Nicole asked. Earlier, she'd talked about meeting up with someone from Tinder, but once she'd heard about Amy's break-up, she'd put her phone away, and her attention was entirely on Amy.

"Do you want Brussels sprouts?" Sierra asked. "They're smothered in cheese and bacon, remember."

Nicole gave her a look. "She doesn't need vegetables at a time like this. You know what they have on the menu? Warm brownies with vanilla ice cream. I'll get you that instead, Amy."

Amy could only nod. She didn't have much of an appetite, but it did sound good.

"So, what happened?" Nicole asked.

Amy gave a brief rundown, and all her new friends listened.

She couldn't help it. She started crying. God, she missed Victor, but she did have wonderful friends in Toronto.

Sierra squeezed her shoulder, and that just made her cry more.

Toronto wasn't a too-good-to-be-true escape from real life.

It *was* her real life.

So many parts of her new life were fantastic. If only the person she cared about most, the person she loved…

Oh, God.

She loved him. That's why it hurt so much.

Rose handed her a tissue as she continued to sob.

Maybe she shouldn't have confronted him. Having Victor, even if she only partially had him, even if their relationship wasn't all it could be…maybe that would be better than nothing.

Instead, she'd opened her big mouth and asked what was wrong.

What if she'd invited him for Thanksgiving? Would things have been different?

She was glad she'd faced her family alone, though. She'd felt like she'd needed that.

But what if…

No, there still would have been problems at one time or another, since he was scared of what they had. He'd wanted so badly to meet her family at Thanksgiving—that had probably frightened him.

He was thirty-nine years old and he was scared of a freaking relationship.

Or maybe relationships got scarier the older you were?

She didn't regret speaking up. She wouldn't settle again, and she knew he could be what she wanted, but he wouldn't let himself be that guy.

And so they were over.

It was terrible, but it was for the best.

There were still tears in her eyes as the waitress set her brownies and ice cream in front of her. The warm brownies smelled amazing.

She slid her spoon into a brownie and put it in her mouth.

Instantly, she was transported back to A Cup of Stars. With Victor.

She refused to let a man ruin brownies for her. She would eat these fucking brownies, and she would enjoy them.

"You're eating like you haven't eaten all day," Sierra said. "Oh my God, you haven't had any food all day, have you?"

Shit, she was right.

Amy continued to stuff brownies into her mouth, as though the faster she ate, the further she could push away the thought of Victor.

Once she'd eaten two-thirds of the dessert, she stopped and looked around. "Does anyone else want some?"

"No, it's okay," Nicole said. "It looks like you need it all yourself."

Amy nodded in relief. "Thanks. The brownies were a great idea."

"Brownies and ice cream have gotten me through many a tough time."

"Let's talk about something other than my broken heart."

The table was silent for a moment, and then Sierra said, "They're making a movie about me, did you hear? They announced the main cast today." She picked up her phone and navigated to a thread on Twitter.

The first photo was of the young actress who'd been cast as Sierra Wu, demon-slayer extraordinaire. The second was of the man who'd play Rebel.

"He's not as handsome as Victor," Amy whispered.

"Shit," Charlotte said. "She's really far gone. You picked the wrong topic, Sierra Wu."

A white guy stopped by their table. "Is your name really Sierra Wu? Like the books?"

Sierra rolled her eyes. "Yeah, and like her, I can slice off someone's head in one swipe."

"Aw, don't be like that," he said. "I was just trying to make conversation."

"And I was trying to end it."

He got the hint and kept moving. When he was seated at a table near the back, he sent them a dark look.

For some reason, that conversation unhinged Amy and she started laughing hysterically, nearly spitting out the last bite of brownie.

She didn't know when she was going to be okay, but at least she could laugh.

When she stepped outside later that evening, there was a candlelight vigil for a raccoon just up the street. He'd been named—perhaps posthumously—Conrad the Second, and there was a bouquet of red roses, multiple cards full of signatures, and a framed photo of a raccoon in a green bin, though that was probably a different raccoon. A small crowd gathered around and sang songs.

It was so bizarre and unexpected.

Yep, this was her city.

"Do you like my costume, Auntie Amy?" Abigail asked.

"Yes, you make a very nice dragon, sweetie," Amy said as she looked at her nieces on her computer screen. Halloween was later in the week, and her nieces wanted to show off their costumes.

"Roar!" Abigail said in a completely non-terrifying voice.

"Daddy, Abigail is being too scary," Mellie whined.

"Then scare her back," Fred said from off-screen. "Dinosaurs are just as scary."

"I'm a stegosaurus," Mellie informed him with a sniff. "Stegosaurus didn't eat other dinosaurs or people. They just ate plants. They weren't scary at all."

"If I'd dressed up as a director like I wanted," Abigail huffed, "I wouldn't need to roar."

"What would you have worn to be a director?" Amy asked.

"Directors just wear ordinary clothes, I think. Maybe glasses. But Mommy told me no one would know what I was, so now I'm a dragon."

"I think dragons are pretty cool."

Amy tried to sound enthusiastic, but it was hard. Nothing was the same without Victor.

Last night, after they'd left Ossington Cider Bar and seen the vigil for the dead raccoon, Sierra had steered her toward an Indian street food place, which did brisk after-midnight business. She said Amy needed to eat more than brownies, and although Amy had pointed out that the cider and brownies and ice cream probably had enough calories for the day, Sierra had convinced her to split an order of samosa chaat. Amy had eaten samosas before, but she'd never had potato samosas cut up and smothered in yogurt and other toppings. It had been delicious, though not as delicious as it would have been a few weeks ago, and she felt disloyal for wishing she were eating with Victor instead.

But she had her friends to help her get through this, and it was nice to talk to her nieces. They always cheered her up.

"What are you, Jessie?" she asked. Her niece's costume looked like it had been constructed out of cardboard and painted yellow. She was also wearing her hardhat.

"Can't you tell?" Jessie said.

"Well, you look like a bulldozer—"

"Yes! That's what I am! A bulldozer. I'm going to bulldoze all the buildings. Roar."

Abigail stuck her nose in the air. "Bulldozers don't roar. Don't you know anything?"

"Daddy, Abigail is being mean."

"Well, maybe it's time to sing your song," Fred said. His face appeared on the screen, and he mouthed "Sorry" to Amy.

"I've been directing them," Abigail said. "They're finally starting to listen. And...action!"

"Jingle bells! Jingle bells!" shouted the girls. "Batman smells! Robin laid an egg..."

After the song, the bulldozer looked at Amy with a frown.

"Auntie Amy, are you okay? You look sad."

"No, she doesn't, you stupid-face," Abigail said.

"Girls..." Fred said.

"Don't worry about me, sweetie." Amy forced a smile to cover the heaviness in her heart. "I'm going to be just fine. I miss you all."

That was okay, though. She couldn't have everything in one place, and she'd made peace with it. She would talk to her family every week and visit when she could, but she belonged in Toronto, even if she didn't have Victor.

"Victor and I broke up," Amy said to Mom on the phone later that day.

"Oh, Amy, I'm so sorry. I know you really liked him."

"Yeah, I did." *But I like myself too much to be with someone who can't give me what I need.* "Even though we weren't together for long, it really hurts."

She started sobbing on the phone. God, she'd been a mess this weekend.

She wished her mom were here to hug her.

"Don't settle," Mom said. "For anything. There will be other men."

The thought of finding another man one day brought Amy no comfort. It was nearly impossible to imagine being with anyone but Victor. Images of their relationship were constantly playing through her mind. The first time they'd kissed in his backyard. Their first date. The beer hall. The time she'd brought her vibrator to his house…

Don't think about that now. You're on the phone with your mother.

After she ended the call, she put on her jacket and headed out to her backyard. She glanced over the fence. No Victor.

That wasn't a surprise. It was a bit cold to be sitting outside now.

She hadn't seen him since they'd broken up. Hopefully living next to him wouldn't be too tough, but there were so many reminders. By springtime, she hoped to be able to sit on the patio without even a smidge of pain.

As she looked up at the back of his house, hugging her arms around herself, her gaze landed on his sunroom. She could see the cacti from here.

And she could see him, too. He seemed to be watering his cacti, his face, still so dear to her, the picture of concentration.

Did his fears have something to do with his brother? Victor had opened up to her about Christian, but she still felt like there were things she didn't understand. If he told her what was up, maybe she could help him, though she wouldn't do all the emotional labor. And he had to talk, rather than hiding from her.

She put a hand to her chest as she headed back inside, her heart twisting painfully.

Her new life was about taking risks, and she'd taken a risk.

No matter how much it hurt, she wouldn't let herself regret it.

And if he changed his mind, she'd hear him out. She did love him so.

Victor turned his mouth away from the phone and coughed.

"Are you sick?" his mother asked.

"No, I'm fine."

"You must be sick. It is almost winter. Flu season. Did you get your flu shot? Make sure you get your flu shot. And make sure you wear your winter jacket."

"That's hardly necessary yet. Toronto isn't as cold as Edmonton."

"Listen to your mother. She knows best. Do you want to get pneumonia?"

"I don't have pneumonia. Something was stuck in my throat."

"Did you eat any of those pineapple candies?" she asked.

"No, I promise I didn't eat anything laced with lead."

"Is Amy looking after you?"

"For the last time," he said. "I'm not sick."

"Why are you getting so mad at your mother? I am just trying to help."

He sighed. "I'm sorry. Amy and I broke up."

"*What?*"

He had to hold the phone far away, lest it damage his hearing. When he brought it close to his ear again, she was still talking.

"…you doing drugs because you are heartbroken? I bet that is why you are coughing."

"I got something caught in my throat!"

"Are you crying? Did Amy dump you because she decided you were too old for her?"

"No, it wasn't like that," he said.

"What is her number? I will call her. Tell her that even though you are an old bachelor, you are still a good catch. Aiyah, your first girlfriend in years!"

"Actually—"

"Wah, don't tell me *you* broke up with *her*. Ivy and Sophia said you were very cute together."

"What else did they tell you?" he asked morosely.

"That you bought her a unicorn mug."

"Yes, I'm aware of that. Sophia sent you the picture."

"Are you using it to collect your tears now?"

"Jesus, Mom. I haven't cried."

Yes, that was true. Barely. He'd almost shed a tear before remembering that the last time he'd cried had been after telling Amy about his brother. That had made his tears dry right up.

"I can hear it. You are very upset, I know."

He put a hand to his head. The painkiller he'd taken earlier hadn't been enough to rid him of this headache. It was only getting worse.

"I know what you are," Mom said. "I learned this new word the other day. You are a masochist. You like feeling pain. Why else would you break up with a woman you love?"

"Why do you think I love her?"

"I can just tell. Silly boy."

Ugh. It was lucky she couldn't read all his thoughts.

They talked for a few more minutes—well, mostly his mother

did the talking, and Victor nodded along, even though she couldn't see him nod.

And then he suddenly asked, "Mom, do you ever think of Christian?"

He regretted the words as soon as he said them.

Of course she thought of her son.

Mom was quiet for a minute, which was unusual, but at last she said, "All the time. You know that."

"You never talk about him."

"I don't want to upset you."

"You wouldn't be upsetting me. It's not like I don't think of him, too."

"Okay, I will talk about him now. He would have thought you are being an idiot."

"Why?"

"About Amy, you idiot!"

Well, wasn't this a fun conversation.

Once he ended the call, he put his phone on the coffee table and sipped his scotch.

It was Tuesday. He and Amy had broken up on Saturday. He'd known he'd have a crappy day or two, but he'd honestly thought that would be it. He'd figured he'd be back to his regular self soon enough.

Instead, he felt even more out of control.

He regarded his glass, then remembered the time Amy had tried his scotch and declared it tasted like a bog, and why would anyone want to drink that?

He downed the rest of it and stared out the window.

Night was falling, and it was gray and wet. Rain made him think of Amy and her ladybug umbrella and polka dot rainboots.

Dear God. This fucking sucked.

He was about to turn away from the window when he saw a red umbrella with black spots. He rubbed his eyes, certain he had to be imagining it.

But, no. It was her.

It felt like his chest was caving in on itself, like he'd cut it with a knife and now his body was giving up on him.

These were exactly the strong feelings he'd been trying to avoid, and now here he was.

His phone rang again and he answered it without looking at the display.

"What the fuck did you do?" Sophia shouted.

"What are you talking about?"

But he knew. His phone call with his mother had ended less than ten minutes ago, but she must have immediately called or texted his sister.

"Your girlfriend, you dumbass! You broke up, even though she's lovely and obviously adored you. What happened?"

Sophia was more than a decade younger than him, and he'd taught her how to tie her shoelaces, but she was terrifying right now.

"I started pulling back," he sighed, "and she decided the relationship was too one-sided. I told her that I couldn't be what she wanted."

"Why were you pulling back?"

"Because I was scared," he said, being stupidly honest.

"Why were you scared? You're a forty-five-year-old man."

"Thirty-nine," he muttered. "I liked my quiet life. She was disrupting it."

But those words were beginning to feel like a lie.

"You were living the most boring life in the world," Sophia said. "You're in the biggest city in Canada and you almost never left your house."

"I go to work every day." He couldn't help defending himself.

"You know what I mean. But with her, you were actually doing things."

"It wasn't *me*, though."

"Why do I feel like I'm the big sister?" Sophia huffed. "She was getting you out of your shell. It was good for you."

"Sophia—"

"Don't worry, I know you're different from me. I get that. You won't stay out clubbing until two in the morning."

He shuddered at the thought.

"But Amy wasn't changing you into someone you're not," Sophia continued. "She was turning you back into yourself."

"I don't know about that."

"Are you going to deny that you were happy with her?"

"No, but—"

"Why don't you want to be happy? Do you feel guilty about being happy when Christian isn't here anymore?"

Her words stunned him.

He was pretty sure she was wrong.

"I don't like strong emotions," he said.

"Are you saying you love her?"

"God, you're annoying."

"So that's a yes." Sophia sighed. "You need to get over your hang-ups. When Amy was around, you practically lit up like a Christmas tree, and I hadn't seen you like that in a long time."

"Thanks for the lovely comparison."

"You're welcome. Now go get her back."

"I'm not…"

But Sophia was already gone.

As he put down his phone, he felt a glimmer of something he refused to call hope. It was for the best that he'd ended things with Amy, wasn't it?

He was a wreck without her, though.

He was actually curling up in a ball on his couch and hugging a pillow because he needed to hug *something*. It was damn embarrassing.

His phone rang again. Ivy.

"What did you do?" she cried.

Apparently, he was talking to every woman in his family tonight.

~

The next night, Victor was sullenly drinking beer at the bar when Jay finally came in and sat down across from him.

"Sorry," Jay said. "Had a minor vomit emergency at home. The little guy is going to be so upset if he misses Halloween."

Amy probably loved Halloween. She'd carve multiple pumpkins and put them on her front porch. She'd probably dress up, too.

Maybe as a really cute ladybug.

Or a really cute unicorn.

Or a really cute...something.

"Hey." Jay snapped his fingers in front of Victor's face. "What's up? Is it that neighbor of yours?"

"We started dating. She even met my sisters. And then we broke up."

He provided a few more details, and Jay seemed as unimpressed as his family had been.

"You think you can avoid all strong emotions," Jay said, "so you broke up with her, and where has that gotten you? You look miserable."

Victor sipped his beer and tried not to look miserable.

"That smile is some scary shit," Jay said. "It'll frighten all the kids tomorrow."

"I'm not giving out candy."

"Why not? You have a house. Don't you usually give out candy?"

"Yeah, but I'm not doing it this year."

"Because you're miserable, missing this woman. So get her back and put an end to your misery. And her misery. I bet she misses you, too, though I can't imagine why. Look, man. Living involves feelings. You can't avoid that. Sometimes it hurts, but it can also be amazing. Love is a good thing, even if everything is all twisted up in your brain. You're hurting right now, but you don't have to."

When his brother had died, Victor hadn't been able to do anything to fix what had happened, and he'd hated that helplessness. That was part of what had overwhelmed him and led to the broken bowl and all those nights when he didn't sleep a wink.

But this wasn't the same. He wasn't helpless. Maybe…

"You think I can get her back?" Victor asked.

"Yeah, I bet you can."

"What should I do?"

"You're the one who knows her, not me. And I can't stay too long to help you brainstorm, unfortunately, since there's a bit of a situation at home."

Jay stayed another twenty minutes, then left Victor there with his second pint of beer.

Yes, he could just talk to Amy. But he wanted to do something big, too. Something to really show her how special she was, and to prove to himself that he'd changed.

He took out his phone and started making a list.

Dress up as a unicorn.

Nope, not happening.

Dress up as a ladybug.

He had to come up with something that didn't involve a costume. He was probably thinking of costumes because it was Halloween tomorrow.

Get her name tattooed on my ass.

Cut the grass shirtless, even though it's nearly November and the grass doesn't need to be cut.

He wished Christian were here. Christian had been good at shit like this.

But even though it hurt that Christian was gone—and it

would always hurt—Victor would never wish that his brother hadn't existed.

That pain was part of life.

And he'd been doing his best to keep his life small in recent years, until Amy had appeared next door.

He wouldn't do that anymore, though.

Christian wouldn't have wanted him to. That's what hit him the hardest. His brother wouldn't have wanted this life for him. If he needed it to cope for a little while, that was one thing, but not for years and years. Victor needed to get himself together and finally move forward.

Amy had met Christian, briefly, all those years ago.

That seemed like a sign.

Except Victor didn't believe in signs.

No, what mattered was that he loved Amy. Even though they weren't together anymore, that hadn't changed. He loved her sunshine personality and her polka dots and her eager smile and the way she twisted her lips when she was trying to understand Fortran.

He loved the way she looked in summer dresses and shorts... and naked. He loved sliding inside her and holding her against his chest.

He loved the way she made him feel, even if it was scary.

And he couldn't push it aside, despite his practice with suppressing emotions. He would learn how to handle it. He wouldn't run away.

She was worth it.

Victor continued making his list, his ideas becoming slightly less ridiculous as he went. When his mom called, he answered.

"Have you fixed everything with Amy?" Mom's voice boomed over the phone. "Is she there with you now? Can I talk to her?"

"Not yet."

"Aiyah! What are you—"

"Don't worry, I'm trying to fix things."

"Good. Maybe you should give her the bath foam I sent you. She will need to de-stress after dealing with *you*."

Well, he'd like to take a bubble bath with Amy, but he wouldn't say that to his mom.

"Okay, I will let you go now," she said. "Good luck. I think you will need it."

"Thanks for your faith in me."

"Don't use that sarcastic tone!" She paused. "Your brother would have wanted you to be happy, you know this, yes?"

"I know," he said quietly.

And suddenly, he had an idea.

He knew a place in Toronto that Amy would love.

[27]

Saturday afternoon, Amy headed to Harbord Coffee Bar. Although she liked trying new things, it was nice to have a favorite place to return to on a regular basis. She'd settled into her life in the city, and as she walked down the street in her jacket, sweater, toque, and scarf, she remembered her first day in Toronto, more than three months ago.

It had been sunny and warm then, but now it was autumn, and most of the leaves had fallen from the trees.

The weather was as bleak as her heart.

Stop it, Amy.

Though she was usually good at looking on the bright side, right now, she was struggling.

She reminded herself of Halloween, two days ago. She loved Halloween. So many children had come to her door, and it had been warm enough here that the kids—at least most of them—hadn't worn snowsuits under their costumes, unlike in Silver River.

"Hi, Amy," Lucy said as she stepped inside. "What can I get for you today?"

"A matcha latte for here, please."

No roll cake or cream puffs for her today. She'd eaten enough Halloween candy, trying to drown her sorrows.

A few minutes later, her matcha latte was ready, and Amy took a seat. She opened up her e-reader, trying to decide what to read next. So many options, and yet it was hard to care.

No, Amy. You will read a book today, and you will enjoy it.

The familiar atmosphere of the coffee shop was rather comforting, and she was taking her first sip of the matcha latte when there was a commotion at the front. Four women burst inside.

Wait a second. Were those…

They came over to Amy's table. Sure enough, it was Sierra, Nicole, Charlotte, and Rose.

"You're coming with us." Charlotte reached for Amy's arm. "I actually put on pants and left the apartment. I will not fail in my mission."

"Where are we going?"

"It's a secret," Rose said, bouncing on her toes.

"Look," Amy said, "I'm happy to go with you in a few minutes, once I finish my latte, but I'd prefer to know what you have in mind."

Nicole gestured to the cab outside. "It's only a short ride. And it's a secret."

Amy's friends were planning a secret something-or-other, presumably to cheer her up. That was kind of them. "Just a few minutes."

"No, we're leaving now." Sierra appeared with a paper to-go cup and poured Amy's matcha latte into it, ruining the pretty latte art. "You can take this with you. Come on."

She and Nicole pulled Amy up, then led her to the door and into the minivan cab. The cab driver seemed to already know where they were going.

Ten minutes later, they stopped beside a park. It was a good size for downtown Toronto, and beyond the off-leash dog area, there was an enormous glass building. A greenhouse? Amy had never seen a greenhouse like this before. It reminded her of Victor's sunroom, but she refused to dwell on that.

A greenhouse was perfect for a bleak day like today.

"Okay, let's go," Nicole said after paying the driver. "You been here before, Amy?"

"No, I never knew this place existed."

"Allan Gardens," Charlotte said. "I've never been here before, either."

"I've been many times," Rose said. "I like coming here in the winter."

They entered the greenhouse. It was warm inside with a light floral scent. They were surrounded by tropical plants, reaching up to the high ceiling. When Amy pulled out her phone to take a picture, Sierra took her arm and led her away.

Amy was confused. What was happening?

"You'll have time for that later," Sierra said.

The next room was a little cooler, and Amy heard running water. There were lots of flowers and a little pond with fish.

Once again, however, Sierra wouldn't let her stay and enjoy it.

Instead, Amy was led into another room, which was warm and very humid. In addition to all the green plants, there were flowers in hanging planters.

"Orchids!" she exclaimed.

They followed a path to the right. There was a little bridge beside a waterwheel and turtles.

"Wow! I..." The words died on her lips.

Because that was when she saw *him*.

Her mouth opened again, but no sound came out.

Victor hadn't seen her, though. He was sitting on a bench, just past the bridge; there were orchids hanging over his head. He was wearing a suit and carrying an enormous bouquet of flowers in a profusion of colors. His foot tapped against the floor as he ran a hand through his hair.

Normally, Amy would be gaping at the orchids and turtles, but now, he was all that mattered. Her friends stayed by the waterwheel, and she went to sit next to Victor on the bench.

"Hey," she said.

"Hey."

Often, he smiled when he saw her, but not today.

"So let me guess." She nodded at the flowers in his hand. "You decided you'd been an ass and want me back."

"Yeah." He chuckled as he gestured to their surroundings. "I thought you'd like it here."

She did. He was good at finding things she liked.

"When you burst into my life," he said, "and I do think 'burst' is the right word, I'm not going to lie. I didn't like it. You interrupted my silence with your laughter and attempts at conversation, even though I was hardly encouraging. But somewhere along the way, those brief conversations, when you'd tell me about what you ate and all the cool things you'd seen in your walks around the city, became the highlight of my day. I'd spend way more time than usual in the backyard, hoping you'd appear." He glanced at the flowers in his hand, and his lips twitched.

"I was determined to be your friend," she said.

"Yes, well. Somehow, it got more complicated. Because you wanted something else, and I did, too. All I could think about was when I would see you again, when I would touch you again. What I could do to make you smile, even if I'm not the sort of guy who's used to making people smile. I wanted you to feel happy and appreciated. I wanted to be with you and absorb your rainbow sprinkles and polka dots." He looked down at her hand, and when she nodded, he took it in his, drawing circles over her palm.

Oh, she'd missed touching him. Missed how it comforted and electrified her all at once.

"For a number of years," he continued, "I've lived a pretty small life. It was my way of coping at first, and it was also the result of losing the one person who'd drag me out, refusing to let me be alone all the time. I do like my peace and quiet, but not every hour of every day. You showed me what I'd been missing in life, and I started actually having fun again. But it was more than that." He swallowed. "I fell in love with you."

She inhaled swiftly at those words.

"It scared the shit out of me," he said. "I didn't like strong emotions I couldn't control. Also, when you didn't invite me for Thanksgiving, I wondered if I was alone in my feelings."

"No, I just—"

"It's okay, I was being insecure. I should have spoken to you, but instead, I pulled away, and you refused to settle—which is good. I want you to have all that you can dream of. I thought that once you were gone…" His voice wobbled. "I could go back to the way things were before. But I was a fucking wreck without you. I can't go back, and I don't want to. I just want you in my life again. I know I screwed up. I know I was stupid. There's no excuse, but I love you, and I'll do anything to make it up to you. You deserve to be cared for and cherished, and I won't hold back anymore. Whatever you want. This is just a start." His voice wobbled again as he handed her the colorful bouquet. "And here's something else."

He pulled a red box out of his jacket. It contained a necklace. Not fancy jewelry: a silver chain with a pendant of two cherries and green leaves. Which could look childish, but somehow this design was very classy and *her*.

"You like it?" he asked.

She nodded, and he fastened it at the back of her neck.

"One last thing." He handed her an envelope.

Inside was a card with an illustration of a man and a woman, hand in hand, looking at a sunrise over the Toronto skyline.

"It's beautiful." From the style, Amy guessed it was one of Sierra's creations.

The card was blank inside, except for the words "love you" and his name.

"Look, I'm not very good with words," he said softly, "even though I've said an awful lot of them in the past five minutes. I'm just so, so sorry, and I won't make the mistake of thinking I should live without you again." He took both of her hands in his. "What do you say?"

"I…I love you, too. None of what you feel is one-sided, I promise. I wasn't looking to fall in love when I moved to Toronto. I wasn't sure when I'd be ready for another relationship. Then I met you, and seeing you became the best part of my day as well. I felt like I could be myself around you, like you got me, even though we're so different, and…" A tear streaked down her face. "So yes, I'd like to be with you and fill your cupboards with a disturbing assortment of cute mugs."

He grinned, and she felt like it was lighting her from within.

"I promise I've moved past my issues," he said, "but of course there will be other struggles in the future, and I promise to communicate and work through everything together."

"Me, too."

"Can I kiss you now?"

When she nodded eagerly, he bent his head and brushed his lips over hers.

Oh, she had missed him so much. And he loved her and she loved him, and it gave her such joy.

She wrapped her arms around him and deepened the kiss.

"We should probably head out," Sierra said.

Amy jerked her head away from Victor's and looked across the small bridge, where her friends were still standing.

"I don't know," Charlotte said. "There might be a twist. Perhaps she's going to slap him."

"Charlotte!" Rose said. "You know, I think you're secretly a romantic, and that's why you want to watch."

"We're leaving." Nicole linked her arm through Charlotte's.

"We'll give them some privacy. I'll text her in twenty-four hours. Maybe they'll have gotten out of bed by then."

Amy blushed as she waved at her friends, then turned back to the man beside her and kissed him some more.

"You're very handsome in that suit," she said. "Should we head home and go to bed?"

"Eventually, but I have other plans first. Let's see the rest of the greenhouse."

He got up and took her hand, and they stood on the bridge to watch the turtles by the waterwheel. Once they'd examined the different varieties of orchids, they walked back to the entrance and headed to the other wing of the greenhouse.

The next room was very green, and to Amy's disappointment, lacking in flowers, but then they reached the last room. A winding path took them past all sorts of cacti. Big, spiky round ones. Tall ones that looked like fuzzy green sausages. One grew along the roof of the greenhouse.

She squeezed Victor's hand.

After they left Allan Gardens, he still had more plans. They went to the restaurant in Yorkville where they'd had their first date. Since it was November, they couldn't sit on the rooftop patio but instead were seated at a table by the window, lit by candlelight.

Amy felt like the luckiest woman.

Because in addition to being freakishly good-looking—and ooh, he was taking off his suit jacket and rolling up his sleeves—Victor was an amazing man who made her feel treasured, and he'd vowed to make this work.

She was giddy with excitement that she got to have dinner again with him.

And dessert.

Rather than gelato, he took her to a nearby chocolate café. The entire menu was dessert.

"I thought you'd like this place," he said.

She'd eaten a good amount at dinner, but that wouldn't get in the way of enjoying something with chocolate. Besides, she was sure she'd need energy for certain *activities* later.

Victor brushed his hand up the inside of her knee and smiled at her, and when the waiter came by, Amy had barely even looked at the menu because they'd spent so much time goofily staring into each other's eyes.

They decided on a waffle topped with three different types of chocolate ice cream, chocolate sauce, strawberry sauce, and fresh berries, and afterward, they each got a cup of tea at a nearby coffee shop, which they took to the giant rock in Yorkville.

There was nobody else on the rock today. They cuddled up next to each other with their tea to warm them. The slightly-wilted bouquet of flowers lay by their feet.

People walked by, going about their evening. The lights of the city surrounded them. Within walking distance, there were countless restaurants, bars, and shops.

Amy looked up. There were only a few stars in the sky, unlike in Silver River.

Then she turned to Victor and snuggled closer to his chest. This was the life she wanted, and she wouldn't feel guilty about it, not one bit.

Yes, here with him, she was home.

IT WAS CHRISTMAS EVE, and Victor Choi was driving his very sensible Honda up north.

Amy was in the passenger's seat. They were going to stay with her family in Silver River for a few days. He'd "met" most of them on Skype—her niece Abigail had given him the disturbing suggestion of getting hearts tattooed on his forehead—but he'd yet to meet her family in person, and admittedly, he was a little nervous.

Amy turned up the Christmas music. Though Victor wasn't much of a Christmas music guy, he liked that she enjoyed it.

There was lots of snow on the side of the road, but it wasn't snowing right now, thankfully. Inside the car, it was toasty and full of holiday spirit. Amy was wearing a sweater with a dinosaur in a Santa hat; Victor's sweater had a rather appalling ginger-bread design.

But according to Amy, this put him in the Christmas spirit, and he wasn't complaining.

They'd gotten back together nearly two months ago, and those months had been amazing. Every day he was bowled over by his love for her and her irrepressible spirit.

And to think, six months ago he'd had no idea what was in store for him. Now he wouldn't have his life any other way, even if it was less orderly and controlled than before. He ate black ice cream dipped in rainbow sprinkles. He drove across town to a restaurant with twenty-four types of poutine.

He nearly stabbed himself in the eye with the unicorn horn on his new unicorn mug.

They also had quiet mornings and evenings together. Lazing in bed, snuggling up and reading, watching movies.

All of it was wonderful.

Okay, the part where he'd almost had to go to the ER wasn't, but still.

"Huh," Amy said. "Charlotte just texted me. Her childhood best friend—who lived next door—found her on Facebook. She's not sure whether to message him back. Obviously, I told her to do it."

"You've had great luck with guys who live next door to you."

"Mm-hmm. I wasn't thinking that they'd date, just catch up, but you're right. Maybe—"

His phone rang, and he pressed a button on his steering wheel to answer.

"Hi, Victor!" his mom said.

"Hi. We're in the car, heading to Silver River."

"Amy is there? Hi, Amy!"

"Hey!" Amy said. "Are you having a good Christmas Eve?"

Mom clucked her tongue. "Ivy and Sophia are making sugar cookies."

"That sounds fun."

"They have taken over my kitchen. Flour and icing every-where. Aiyah!"

Amy's laughter filled the car, and Victor couldn't help smiling.

"But that wasn't why I called," Mom said. "I want to tell you to be careful on the road. Do not hit a moose. Or a deer. Or a bear."

"I understand your concerns," Victor said, "and I will be careful. Though I think bears are hibernating at this time of year."

"You never know! That's what they want you to think. Then they sneak up and attack your car, looking for Christmas treats."

"I'll be sure to keep that in mind, thanks."

"You are using that *tone* with me again. Amy, isn't he using that tone?"

"Yes, I'll be sure to scold him later."

Victor suspected this "scolding" would involve kissing, but he didn't say that.

"I am looking forward to seeing you at the Lunar New Year, Mrs. Choi," Amy said.

"Ah, yes. Me, too. It is not every day Victor brings home a woman. We will have lots to talk about."

They spoke for a few more minutes, Victor keeping an eye out for Winnie-the-Pooh or Paddington, just in case they popped out of the woods and demanded gingerbread. Perhaps they'd try to eat his sweater.

He ended the call, and then it was just him and Amy again.

He'd given her a small present before they'd left: the cherry apron she'd admired many months back. In return, she'd given him a bottle of extra-peaty scotch.

But he had more things to give her when they returned home, such as the small velvet box hiding in the bottom drawer of his desk.

He hadn't decided when or how he'd propose, but it would be soon. He was Amy's, and he knew he wanted to spend his life with her.

They'd wander Toronto and cities around the world, eating lots of great food together.

He'd cut the grass shirtless whenever she wanted. Maybe he'd even shovel the snow without a shirt…

Nah, that was a little much.

He didn't know exactly where life would lead them and how

many colorful mugs he'd have in his cupboard a year from now, but he was looking forward to a little excitement, rather than trying his best to preserve his life alone.

"I can't wait for everyone to meet you," Amy said, "but I'm going to give you the best Christmas present tonight, when it's just the two of us in my old bedroom."

He glanced over at Amy in her dinosaur Christmas sweater. She was utterly beautiful.

"Is it sex?" he murmured. "I bet it's sex."

"You'll just have to wait and see. But I'll give you a hint: that gingerbread sweater is going to look most excellent on the floor."

"Better than it looks on me, that's for sure."

They shared a laugh as they drove into their future together.

ACKNOWLEDGMENTS

Thank you to my editor, Latoya C. Smith, as well as my beta readers—Kate Pearce, Alana Delacroix, and Aaliyah Jackson—for their help with this book. The cover was created by Flirtation Designs.

Thank you also to Toronto Romance Writers, plus my family, for all their support.

Jackie Lau decided she wanted to be a writer when she was in grade two, sometime between writing "The Heart That Got Lost" and "The Land of Shapes." She later studied engineering and worked as a geophysicist before turning to writing romance novels. Jackie lives in Toronto with her husband, and despite living in Canada her whole life, she hates winter. When she's not writing, she enjoys gelato, gourmet donuts, cooking, hiking, and reading on the balcony when it's raining.

To learn more and sign up for her newsletter,
visit jackielaubooks.com.

Cider Bar Sisters Series

Her Big City Neighbor

His Grumpy Childhood Friend

Her Pretend Christmas Date (novella)

Kwan Sisters/Fong Brothers Series

Grumpy Fake Boyfriend

Mr. Hotshot CEO

Pregnant by the Playboy

Holidays with the Wongs Series

A Match Made for Thanksgiving

A Second Chance Road Trip for Christmas

A Fake Girlfriend for Chinese New Year

A Big Surprise for Valentine's Day

Baldwin Village Series

One Bed for Christmas (prequel novella)

The Ultimate Pi Day Party

Ice Cream Lover

Man vs. Durian

Chin-Williams Series

Not Another Family Wedding

He's Not My Boyfriend